Molly he

"Let's call a truce for the next thirty days," she said. "Agreed?"

Hudson reached out and shook her hand. "Agreed," he said. He was so surprised by the unexpected feelings between them that he quickly let go of her hand.

Molly's eyes widened. Whatever this was, she'd felt it too. He wasn't imagining things.

"I've got to go," she said, quickly putting on her parka and heading toward the door.

"I should get back to it myself," Abel said. "I'll walk you out, Molly. See you soon, Hudson."

"Bye," Hudson said in a low voice. He was feeling overwhelmed by the whirlwind events of his first day back in town. Once the door closed behind them, his mind began to race with questions.

The thought of working side by side with Molly at Humbled was a bit disorienting. Just a few hours ago she hadn't even wanted him in the shop, yet now she would have to welcome him with open arms.

Belle Calhoune is a *New York Times* bestselling author. She grew up in a small town in Massachusetts. Married to her college sweetheart, she is raising two lovely daughters in Connecticut. A dog lover, she has one mini poodle and a black Lab. Writing for the Love Inspired line is a dream come true. Working at home in her pajamas is one of the best perks of the job. Belle enjoys summers in Cape Cod, traveling and reading.

Books by Belle Calhoune

Love Inspired

Serenity Peak

Her Alaskan Return
An Alaskan Blessing
His Secret Alaskan Family
An Alaskan Christmas Prayer

Home to Owl Creek

Her Secret Alaskan Family
Alaskan Christmas Redemption
An Alaskan Twin Surprise
Hiding in Alaska
Their Alaskan Past
An Alaskan Christmas Promise

Alaskan Grooms

An Alaskan Wedding
Alaskan Reunion
A Match Made in Alaska

Visit the Author Profile page at LoveInspired.com.

AN ALASKAN CHRISTMAS PRAYER

BELLE CALHOUNE

If you purchased this book without a cover you should be aware that this book is stolen property. It was reported as "unsold and destroyed" to the publisher, and neither the author nor the publisher has received any payment for this "stripped book."

LOVE INSPIRED®
INSPIRATIONAL ROMANCE

ISBN-13: 978-1-335-62128-3

An Alaskan Christmas Prayer

Copyright © 2025 by Sandra Calhoune

All rights reserved. No part of this book may be used or reproduced in any manner whatsoever without written permission.

Without limiting the author's and publisher's exclusive rights, any unauthorized use of this publication to train generative artificial intelligence (AI) technologies is expressly prohibited.

This is a work of fiction. Names, characters, places and incidents are either the product of the author's imagination or are used fictitiously. Any resemblance to actual persons, living or dead, businesses, companies, events or locales is entirely coincidental.

For questions and comments about the quality of this book, please contact us at CustomerService@Harlequin.com.

® is a trademark of Harlequin Enterprises ULC.

Love Inspired	HarperCollins Publishers
22 Adelaide St. West, 41st Floor	Macken House, 39/40 Mayor Street Upper,
Toronto, Ontario M5H 4E3, Canada	Dublin 1, D01 C9W8, Ireland
www.LoveInspired.com	www.HarperCollins.com

Printed in Lithuania

Recycling programs for this product may not exist in your area.

For by grace are ye saved through faith;
and that not of yourselves: it is the gift of God.
—*Ephesians* 2:8

For my friend, Angela Anderson.
Thanks for being such an amazing cheerleader.

Chapter One

Molly Truitt loved nothing more than opening up Humbled, her bookstore-café, each and every morning. Main Street in Serenity Peak, Alaska, was quiet this time of the day as she drove her cherry red truck, Bessie, into town. Molly had arisen as the sun was rising over the horizon, casting its golden glow over the majestic mountains. This time of year was the best season of all, with the whole downtown area decked out with Christmas decorations. Festive wreaths. Twinkling lights and garlands. Holly and mistletoe. Candy canes and glittering ornaments. And, on the town green, a stately balsam fir that would be lit up at the annual town festival. Just the thought of it caused pure joy to course through her veins.

Oh, there was so much to look forward to during the most wonderful time of the year. Caroling with the church choir. Christmas cards, and candles shining brightly at the midnight church service. Sugar cookies and peppermint hot cocoa would be served daily at the café, along with chocolate yule logs and eggnog. She had already bought a number of presents, and she couldn't wait to wrap them. Wrapping gifts was one of her favorite things about Christmas, second only to the joy the presents brought to her loved ones.

It was also such a wonderful time to celebrate the birth of Christ and lean into her faith.

She slid her truck into her usual parking spot and headed toward Humbled. Molly let out a sigh of contentment as she opened up the shop and stepped inside. She just knew this was going to be a amazing day. Molly could feel it in her bones. She couldn't wait until the first customer walked through the doors.

She picked up a piece of chalk and began to write her favorite Bible verse, Psalm 118:24, on the chalkboard. *This is the day which the Lord hath made. We will rejoice and be glad in it.* Molly stood back and admired her handiwork before heading behind the counter and turning on the espresso machine. All she wanted to do was sit down at a table and drink a coffee, indulge in one of her favorite books and eat a delectable apple turnover. It was absolutely wonderful to spend some time with herself before devoting herself to the shop.

Molly found a seat at a table where the sunlight streamed in and she could sit back and relax until it was time to open the place. Everything was in order for today's menu. She'd taken care of all the pastries with the help of her top baker, Estelle. They always prepped the night before for the next day. She didn't know what she would do without the older woman. She was always pitching in and making Molly's job less hectic. It wasn't easy running a bookstore and a café, although she truly loved the hustle and bustle of owning a beloved business. Humbled had taken off with the townsfolk at an incredible pace, making it a profitable enterprise for Molly. To say that the family business was her pride and joy was an understatement. Molly had been running it for almost five years now. And Humbled had been in business for five decades.

Years ago, Molly had fostered other dreams. College hadn't worked out for her, and a failed relationship with her boyfriend, Will, had made her feel a bit hopeless. She had believed that Will was "the one" before things had fallen apart. But then everything changed when she took over running the shop. Suddenly she had a purpose.

She didn't take Humbled for granted. Molly always took time to count her blessings. She only wished Granny Eva was around to witness the popularity of Humbled. Her grandmother had conceived the idea of merging her love of pastries, coffee and books into a small café where books were scattered in every nook and cranny of the place. Molly herself had come up with the idea of having two shops in the same building—one half bookstore, one half a café. Her idea had been well received by the townsfolk.

The place had come a long way since the early years. Molly had made it her mission to modernize Humbled while retaining its charm and whimsy. Considerable work had been done to add extra space to the structure. It was open and airier, with more square footage. The kitchen had been completely gutted then rebuilt from the ground up. When customers walked in they were greeted at the bakery counter where they could place an order for takeout or choose to sit down at the café on the right side. To the left of the front counter was the entrance to the bookstore. There was no door between the shops, allowing for an open, free flowing layout.

In so many ways, Humbled was a tribute to her sweet, hardworking Gran. She couldn't help but wish Gran was still around to experience it. In her mind's eye, she could easily picture Gran sitting at a table reading one of her favorite Agatha Christie books and drinking a cup of chamomile tea.

The tinkling of the bell above the front door startled her out of her thoughts. She had inadvertently left the door unlocked earlier. A tall figure with dark hair stepped inside. The man was handsome with a lean build. He was around her age, wearing a gray suit that seemed a little bit out of place here in town. He had tourist written all over him.

"I'm sorry," she said, glancing at the clock on the wall. "We don't open for twenty more minutes."

"Good morning, Molly," the man said with a nod. "It's been a long time."

Huh? Did she know him? He didn't look at all familiar. Serenity Peak was the sort of town where everyone knew one another's names.

The man rested his palm on his chest. "Oh, you've wounded me. How soon we forget."

His eyes were the most unique shade of hazel. She'd seen those eyes before, years and years ago. Time changed a lot of things, but eyes weren't one of them.

"H-Hud? Is that you?" she asked, surprise registering in her voice.

He nodded as a wide grin spread across his face. "It's me, in the flesh. Your old buddy who used to yank on your pigtails in class."

Hudson Doherty! The memory of him tugging on her hair arose, feeling like a thorn in her side. He'd been a bit of a pest back then, but since their grandmothers had been best friends she'd learned to tolerate him. And yet, in their teen years their dynamic had shifted to something more tender. A romance. Until he'd up and left Serenity Peak without a word of goodbye to attend college. At the time, she'd been wounded by the fact that their brief relationship had clearly meant nothing to Hud.

Her mind was whirling trying to uncover how many

years stood between them. He'd had a serious glow up if she was being completely honest. Hud was very easy on the eyes. The last ten years had changed him.

She was practically speechless. He had grown up with her in Serenity Peak but had moved to Boston to attend college roughly a decade ago. She hadn't seen him in years. But from what she'd heard from his family, Hudson was some sort of big shot.

"Wh-what are you doing here?" she asked. He hadn't even come back to town for his grandmother's funeral three years ago, which had shocked a lot of folks. Their grandmothers had passed away within six months of one another, which had been poignant. She'd heard a rumor that Hud had missed his flight back home, yet he hadn't bothered to come at all to be with his family. She hadn't wanted to judge, but it had been shocking. "I'm surprised to see you back in Serenity Peak."

He shoved his hands in his pockets and began looking around the café, seemingly oblivious to her question. Hudson let out a low whistle. "This place looks fantastic. You really reinvented it from its original state. The color scheme is great."

A feeling of pride burst inside her chest. Hudson noticing all the hard work she'd put into Humbled felt gratifying. It had taken blood, sweat and tears to turn this place into such a stunning establishment. "It's been such a wonderful experience modernizing this place while still keeping my grandmother's vision intact."

Hudson frowned at her, his mouth twisting. "*Your* grandmother? I think my grandmother had a big hand in the concept for Humbled. Not that your family has acknowledged it, but she was an equal partner in conceiving the idea for the business."

"That's not true. Sure, they were close friends who shared ideas, but it wasn't a partnership." The words flew out of her mouth. She wasn't going to sit here and allow Hudson to revise history. Clearly, he was toying with her.

His hazel eyes glinted. "I honestly think you might believe that, but there's documents that suggest otherwise."

Molly knit her brows together. He was talking in riddles. She had forgotten how infuriating he could be. "Hudson, I have no idea what you're talking about, and frankly, I don't want to know."

"You can't continue to stick your head in the sand," Hudson said, his tone taking on a superior air. "I thought you were a businesswoman."

"Where is all of this coming from?" she asked, throwing her hands in the air and letting out a frustrated sound.

"Molly, don't hate me but…" Hudson's voice trailed off.

"Why would I ever hate you?" she asked, perplexed by his comment and the way he had randomly shown up at her place of business after all these years.

He dug into his bag and pulled out a large envelope, which he extended to her. As soon as she took it, he said, "You've been served, Molly Truitt."

She looked down at the envelope in her hands. "That isn't funny," she said, scowling at him. "I see you're still pulling pranks all these years later."

Hudson had a little smirk on his face that made her want to toss him out of Humbled on his ear. What was going on with him? He was playing some messed-up, annoying game, which was reminiscent of his childhood antics.

"This isn't a joke. You've been served by yours truly," he said, puffing out his chest.

Hud's statement caused a chill to pass through her. She

had no idea what was going on, but a wave of panic enveloped her. He seemed way too gleeful for her liking.

She fumbled with the envelope's clasp then pulled out the papers with jerky hands. Molly shook her head back and forth, confusion sweeping over her as the words jumped out at her from the pages. Her heart thumped wildly as the words *Humbled*, *lawsuit* and *ownership* jumped out at her. Molly dragged her gaze up to meet his. His eyes were void of any meaningful expression.

"What in the world?" she exploded, her cheeks warming. "This is outrageous even for you."

"Ouch. That's not very nice. I thought we were old friends," he said dryly. He winked at her. "Matter of fact, I even thought you might be carrying a torch for me."

"You thought wrong, Hudson Doherty! You should be ashamed of yourself. What right do you have to try and claim my shop?" She shook the papers, causing a loud rippling sound. "This lawsuit isn't worth the paper it's written on."

Hudson let out a chuckle. "You couldn't be more wrong. The paperwork is legit. I'm suing you for co-ownership of this delightful shop. And there really isn't anything you can do about it."

Molly's complexion had paled, and her mouth hung open. A look of shock was etched on her fine features. If he wasn't so angry about the situation, he might feel a little guilty about blindsiding her. Yet after what her family had done, Hudson had zero regrets. It was up to him to uphold his grandmother's legacy and fight for justice. That was the reason he'd traveled all the way from Boston to Alaska, taking two commercial planes and a small seaplane to reach his hometown. It had been kind of cool to run into his childhood pal, Caden Locke, who had been his pilot on the seaplane from Anchorage to Serenity Peak.

He glanced at her again. Molly Truitt was a good-looking woman. Although she seemed plain at first glance, on further inspection, she was lovely. Blue eyes, bow-shaped lips and striking features. Small freckles dotted her cheeks. Everything came together to create a stunning visual. Locks of brown hair framing her face completed the picture. A little over a decade ago, during their senior year of high school, he'd fallen like a ton of bricks for her. They had dated for a few months. Once he'd realized that she was a distraction to his future and his college plans, Hud had beat a fast path out of Serenity Peak. He hadn't handled the situation well at all, but it had been a form of self-preservation. Every now and then he found himself wondering what might have been if he hadn't left.

"I really think you should take a few minutes to look over the paperwork. Actually, I'll do you a solid and give you the abridged version," he told her.

Molly folded her arms across her chest. Her expression was mutinous. "Go ahead," she said. Hudson wasn't sure, but he was fairly certain she'd let out a little growl.

"Humbled as a concept was conceived by *our* grandmothers, emphasis on *our*. Two people. Not one," he said. "With all due respect, your gran didn't have the legal right to leave it to your family in her will."

"Of course she did," Molly said, sounding heated. "I won't deny that your gran served as a sounding board, but she was a friend, not a co-creator. And never an owner."

Just hearing the words come out of Molly's mouth made steam come out of his ears. She was totally minimizing his grandmother's contributions. He clenched his fists at his side.

He did his best not to respond to her statement. Being emotional wouldn't serve him well at all. Facts won cases. Cold, hard facts. And he had a lot of information and witness accounts to bolster his lawsuit. He had done his research, and the conclusion he'd reached was compelling. This property didn't exclusively belong to the Truitt family.

"Well, that remains to be seen, doesn't it?" He shrugged. "A court will have to decide what the truth is."

"Truth? Clearly, you don't have a great relationship with the truth," she snapped. "Otherwise you wouldn't have shown up like a bad penny spinning fanciful tales."

Don't lash out, he reminded himself. If nothing else, he needed to act somewhat professional. His family still lived here, and he didn't want his mother getting on his case. As it was, this entire matter was going to come as a complete shock to all of them, with the exception of his grandfather.

"Molly, I know this isn't easy, but I promise that I'll make it as uncomplicated for you as possible. Believe it or not, I'm one of the good guys." And he really was. This entire pursuit was in his grandmother Lillian's honor. She deserved to have a legacy, and it wasn't fair that the Truitt family had hidden her contributions and assumed complete ownership of Humbled. It wasn't right to have cheated his grandmother in such a conniving way.

"I cannot believe your nerve." At this point, steam was practically coming out of Molly's ears. "You show up out of nowhere, serve me with legal papers, act as if you have some right to my shop and then act as if you're some knight in shining armor riding to my rescue."

Hudson quirked his mouth. "Trust me, I'm trying to be nice."

Molly scoffed. "If this is any evidence of you trying to be pleasant, you need to go back to charm school."

Tension crackled in the air between them. He should have known this would turn acrimonious. Even as a kid, Molly had never been able to budge on a single issue. There was no way in the world she would ever give him an inch in this situation. Which was why he had to take matters into his own hands. He'd chosen to come to Humbled as his first stop because he hadn't wanted another day to go by without asserting his claim.

"Something smells good in here," he said, trying to lighten the mood.

Molly didn't respond. She simply scowled. Not that he could really blame her. Being served with legal papers was enough to ruin a person's mood.

Hudson jerked his head in the direction of her espresso. "How about you make me a coffee on the house?" he asked, grinning. "And toss in a scone while you're at it."

Molly took a step toward him. "How about I push you into the freezing waters of Kachemak Bay?" she asked.

Hudson threw his head back and let out a hearty laugh. Molly was still as opinionated as she'd been as a child yet a bit more brash. Something told him she wasn't kidding around. If she could, Molly would dunk him in ice-cold Alaskan waters and not think twice about doing so.

"Now Molly, that's downright unfriendly of you. Has the town motto changed in the last few years?" He made a face and said, "We're all family in Serenity Peak. Wasn't that it?"

Molly met his gaze head on. Her eyes had a steely glint to them. "No, we still abide by that credo, unless of course a snake comes slithering back into town trying to stir up trouble."

He quirked his mouth. "Something tells me I'm not getting service this morning, which is a tad disappointing."

His stomach was grumbling, and he really loved his morning cup of joe. He'd come straight here after getting off the seaplane rather than heading over to his family's place.

"Or any other morning. This is my establishment, and since you've been MIA for a long time now, you have no idea how hard I've worked to rejuvenate this place." Tears pooled in her eyes, causing his heart to sink. Even though he knew what he was doing was well within his family's legal rights, he didn't want to wound Molly. In truth, he wanted this situation handled as expeditiously as possible. For everyone's benefit.

He reached out to console her, touching her arm. "Molly, please don't cry."

She slapped his hand away. "Don't you dare. I'm not buying your contrition for one single moment. You came here looking for trouble, and you found it."

He fought against a rising tide of frustration. Molly was a spirited young woman who was either foolish or being willfully ignorant. "I'm simply trying to protect my gran's legacy and get what rightfully belongs to my family. There's no shame in that."

"If you think I'm going to allow you to steal my business out from under me, you've got another think coming." She pointed her finger toward the door. "I'd like you to get out of my shop. Now!"

He held up his hands as she advanced toward him. "Okay. I heard you. I'm going. But I'll be back," he said, heading toward the door. "After all, half of this place belongs to *my* family."

She yanked the door open for him with a flourish. He stood in the entryway and turned back toward her. "I really do like what you've done to the place. It has a lot of charm."

Molly shook her head, her brown locks swinging around

her shoulders. Her features were tightly drawn, her mouth turned downward. "I know one thing for certain. If your Nana were still alive, she'd be ashamed of you and what you're trying to do. Shame on you." The door slammed behind him, and suddenly he was outside in the cold, reeling from her parting comment. Her words cut deep, serving as a reminder that he carried around a great deal of shame. Despite the festive decorations adorning all of the shops on Main Street, Hudson wasn't experiencing the holiday spirit. All of a sudden, he felt as deflated as a popped balloon. Hudson had lost his jobs as a marketing exec, his lease in Back Bay would soon expire and he was as close to being broke as he'd ever been in his adult life.

He wasn't looking forward to explaining all of this to his family. For all he knew, they might be just as upset with him as Molly had been. He had chosen to serve her the paperwork before they could try and talk him out of it.

For most of his life, Hud had been the black sheep of the Doherty family. He was different from them in a way he'd always struggled to put his finger on. Some instinct told him that his status wasn't going to change anytime soon.

Chapter Two

"Good morning," Molly said in her cheeriest voice to each and every customer who came into the shop, trying her best to push all memories of Hud out of her mind. Although Molly wanted nothing more than to wallow in her current situation, a steady stream of customers began to walk through the door right after Hudson's departure. She plastered a welcoming smile on her face and went about the business of being a shop owner. She did her best to quiet the anxious voice inside of her.

Wasn't it just like Hudson to leave a firestorm in his wake? He had always been the type of kid who threw the dynamite then ran in the other direction. She had to wonder if he would be sticking around town to see this through or if he would bail and head back to Boston.

Please Lord, let Hudson head back to the Northeast and leave my shop alone.

Everything had been going so well, like a well-oiled machine.

"Hey, Molly. This place is packed today." The familiar sound of her best friend's voice washed over her like a warm rain. Skye Campbell had been her closest pal since nursery school. They had always been inseparable. In the past few years, things had changed a bit in each of their lives, with Molly running Humbled and Skye being newly married to Ryan and mother to an adopted child, Lula. They had been blessed with a newborn baby, Rosalie. From what Molly could sense, Skye's life was idyllic. She knew that Skye had been through a lot with her former fiancé, Tyler, calling off their wedding and some turmoil over the adoption of Lula, but she'd gone through the storms and found true happiness.

What Molly wouldn't give to experience such real, enduring love. All she had were shattered dreams of what might have been with Will and a few months of being romanced by Hud. She wasn't where she wanted to be in her personal life. Not by a long shot.

Skye was grinning at Molly and radiating a contented vibe. What Molly wouldn't give to be feeling upbeat rather than in despair. She had no idea what she was going to do. Lawsuits were expensive. Her stomach was in knots.

"How's it going?" Skye asked, sounding chirpy.

Upon hearing the question from her best friend, Molly burst into tears. Try as she might, there was just no stemming the tide of emotion rising up inside of her.

"What's wrong, Molly?" Skye immediately asked, rushing behind the counter and placing her arm around her.

Molly buried her face in her hands and let out a sob. "Oh, Skye. This has been the worst morning. I-I'm just beside myself." She turned away so none of the customers would notice her weeping.

"Let's go in the back where it's quiet," Skye suggested. "I'll ask Estelle to cover the counter for you."

Molly nodded and made her way to her small office in the back. She shut the door behind her, needing a few moments of solitude. Deep breaths, she reminded herself.

Seconds later, Skye entered the room, her usually placid expression etched with concern.

"Estelle is covering you, and Vinny is in the bookstore," Skye explained. Estelle Van Dusen and Vinny Clark both worked for her at Humbled. Vinny was a popular guy in his late twenties while Estelle was in her sixties. They were both wonderful employees who she counted on to keep the shop running smoothly. Humbled wasn't an overnight success story. It had only taken off after she'd spent countless hours reinventing the business. She had begun the process five years ago, prior to losing Gran.

"So, what's happened to make you so upset?" Skye asked, worry radiating from her eyes.

Molly reached out and squeezed Skye's hand. "Thanks for handling things. I've had quite a shock." Skye didn't say anything but waited for her to continue.

"I'm being sued for ownership of Humbled." She rummaged in her top desk drawer and pulled out the paperwork Hud had given her earlier.

Skye's eyes widened as she reached for the pages then flipped through them. After a few moments, she swung her gaze upward. "Hudson Doherty is suing you?" Skye asked. Her best friend seemed to be just as stunned as Molly had been.

"One and the same," Molly confirmed, nodding her head while wiping tears away from her cheeks. "Just showed up here talking nonsense about his grandmother being a co-creator of Humbled. Lillian was besties with my gran, but I've never heard a word about her having a hand in the business. I know there were some disagreements between them over the years, but I never heard it was about the business." Sure, they had probably tossed ideas around, but what Hud was suggesting was a stretch.

"And if what he's saying is true, then why did he wait all this time to make noise about it?" Skye asked. "Isn't there a statute of limitations?"

"That's a great point." Leave it to Skye to bring up things she'd overlooked. As the daughter of Abel Drummond, a successful businessman and owner of a local company, Sugar Works, Skye was very savvy. She ran the family's general store, Sugar's Place, and was involved in numerous aspects of the business.

Molly shrugged. "It was totally out of the blue. Hud showed up before I had even opened up for the day." Now that she could think straight, Molly had so many questions. Had he just arrived in Serenity Peak?

Skye appeared as shocked as she felt. "I can't believe he's back. And trying to stir up a hornet's nest in the process."

Molly scoffed. "Oh, I can believe it. Hud has always liked to push buttons. He was constantly doing that when we were growing up."

Skye chewed her lip. "You're right about that. But he's a grown man now. What's the point of all this?"

"I don't know," she admitted. Her mind was whirling with dozens of thoughts. What would her family say? And her granddad, Phineas, who had run the shop alongside her gran. If there was any truth to what Hud was claiming, surely he would know.

"Molly, I think you need to talk to an attorney. And show them this paperwork."

She sank down into a wooden chair, her legs feeling like jelly. "I—I don't have that type of money. Things have only just started to financially take off at the shop."

"I understand that, but don't worry. We'll figure things out," Skye said, her voice soothing. "I can ask my father for some names of local attorneys. And then we'll go from there. Okay?"

The *we* in Skye's words didn't escape Molly's notice. That was the type of friend Skye was. She was in this with Molly, which instantly made her outlook change. She wasn't going down without a fight. Hudson was going to see that she wasn't a pushover.

"We will," she said fiercely. "If Hud thinks he can waltz back into town and take what's mine, I'm going to show him just how wrong he is."

After leaving Humbled, Hud knew he had to make his way to his family's compound as fast as possible. Word would quickly spread all over town about him being back in Serenity Peak, as well as his pending lawsuit against Molly. He knew that his family would be confused by his sudden appearance in town as well as shocked by his actions. Meeting up with his family wasn't going to be easy, especially once they discovered the reason for his return. Now at least, it was a done deal and they couldn't pressure him to stand down.

They weren't the sort of people to court trouble, even if it was justified. Hud would just have to convince them that his actions had been based on a desire to uphold Lillian Doherty's legacy. He wasn't trying to hurt Molly or the Truitt family. That might be a casualty of his legal battle, but it wasn't anything he wanted. Memories of Molly being his childhood buddy gently washed over him. They had been as thick as thieves until their teenaged years, when things had turned romantic. Everything had changed almost overnight when he'd decided to head off to Boston for college, leaving sweet Molly behind. Hud shook off the nostalgic feelings. From this point forward, he needed to focus on the matter at hand, which was establishing co-ownership of Humbled.

He let out a chuckle as he got behind the wheel of his rented vehicle. He could navigate the trip blindfolded if need be. Every single bend in the road Hudson knew by heart. Some things a person never forgot, like their first kiss or getting their driver's license.

Hud rolled down the window and allowed the crisp Alaskan wind to flow over him. He took a deep breath and inhaled the pristine air. It was nice to be back, despite the awkward circumstances and the bittersweet memories of his gran. He steeled himself against the reality that although Lillian would be everywhere around him, she would no longer be physically present. Hud ached at the harsh reality that he wouldn't be able to hug her or give her a kiss on the cheek. Would her signature scent of lavender still fill the air at the house? This was uncharted territory for him. His grandmother had been as constant as the North Star. He prayed that his family wouldn't bring up the fact that he'd missed her funeral. It was still something that devastated him. It was always best for him to stuff down those feelings rather than dwell on the fact that he hadn't been able to say goodbye to his gran.

He drove toward the mountains, becoming a little choked up as his family's property drew closer. Doherty's Christmas Tree Farm. The hunter green-and-gold sign rose up to greet him like an old friend. His folks hadn't changed the sign since before he was born. Festive wreaths hung by the wooden gates, and he knew the scent of balsam fir trees would be drifting around him.

The tree farm had been in existence for generations of Doherty's. His parents had been running the place for decades with the help of his grandfather, Bert. The establishment was well-known here in Serenity Peak. His younger siblings, Drew, Anna and Theo, were all helpers when they were available. With the Christmas season in full swing, Hud imagined that his family was being inundated with orders.

There was nothing that made folks smile wider than a beautiful Christmas tree ready for adornment. Hud grinned as he pulled up near the house, put the truck in Park and stepped down from the vehicle. The familiar scent of Christmas trees rose to his nostrils, serving as a reminder that he was finally back home. He was surprising himself by being emotional about it. Hud didn't consider himself to be someone who was affected by people, places or circumstances. He'd always prided himself on being stoic. Had he even cried about losing his gran?

Hudson looked over at the sprawling property that had been in his family longer than the tree farm. The holiday season had always been a highlight in his life, going all the way back to when he was a little kid. A festive vibe was ever present at his family's property.

Growing up, his family of six had lived here with their grandparents. It had always been a home bustling with activity, as well as lots of love. As he stood on the doorstep, a hundred different questions raced through his mind. Would they welcome him with open arms? Was anyone still holding it against him that he'd missed Gran's funeral? Guilt and shame had kept him away, but no one knew that. Four years was a long time to be away from one's family. They had visited him in Boston on several occasions, even though his dad hadn't accompanied them. Video calls and phone calls had filled in the gaps.

He didn't bother knocking but simply turned the knob and walked into the house. Saturday morning meant everyone should be home. The smell of a cooked meal wafted throughout the corridor from the kitchen. If he knew his mother at all, she was probably making a roast or Irish stew in the slow cooker. He kicked off his shoes and placed them on the mat by the door. He then shrugged off his suit jacket and loosened his shirt, taking off the tie. The Doherty clan wouldn't recognize him with a suit and tie on. When Hud was at home, he was a sweater and jeans kind of guy.

He walked with soft steps toward the kitchen, stopping in the doorway as sounds of Christmas music flooded through a Bluetooth speaker, creating a festive atmosphere. "Chestnuts roasting on an open fire," Hud sang the verse that he'd known by heart since he was small. At the sound of his voice, his mother whirled around from the stove to face him. At the same time, Anna let out a squeal, and Drew stood up from his seat and charged toward him while letting out a whoop of joy. Hudson found himself on the receiving end of huge bear hugs and kisses on his cheek by his mother. Leticia Doherty had always been an emotional person, and this instance was no different. Tears streamed unbidden down her cheeks as she said his name over and over again.

When they finally let go of him, Hudson was blinking away his own tears. He hadn't quite expected to feel this amount of emotion rising to the surface. It threatened to overwhelm him.

Leticia reached out and placed his face between her hands. "My handsome boy has become even more good-looking," she gushed. Both Drew and Anna chuckled in response.

"Aww, Mom. You're just the tiniest bit biased, aren't you?" Hudson asked. He was getting a kick out of how excited everyone was to see him. All this time, he'd had a knot in his stomach.

Moments later, his grandfather came rushing into the kitchen. "What's going on? Is something wrong?" he asked, a perplexed expression stamped on his wizened features.

"Grandad," Hudson said, watching as his grandfather's features softened and his eyes welled with tears. At almost six feet tall, Bert Doherty stood eye to eye with him.

"Hud," Bert said, quickly closing the distance between them and pulling Hudson in for a tight hug. As always, the scent of sandalwood hovered around the older man. "Let me look at you," he said once he released him from the embrace.

"Doesn't he look like a movie star?" his mother gushed. With slightly graying hair that hung past her shoulders and sky-blue eyes, she was a striking woman.

"Sure does," Bert agreed with a nod. "And mighty spiffy in his shirt and slacks."

Hudson chuckled. "I'm going to get a swollen head listening to all of you." He would never admit it, but being fawned over felt good. His life in Boston had been busy, work wise, and although he had a large friend circle he'd always felt lonely. Working on marketing campaigns for large companies had paid him handsomely and boosted his name in the industry. For a lengthy period of time that had been enough to keep him away from home.

"Don't worry," Drew said, slapping him on the shoulder. "I've already established myself as the good-looking one in the family." At twenty-five, Drew was a few years younger than Hudson, but the two shared an uncanny resemblance.

"Yeah right," eight-year-old Anna said with a snort, earning herself a tweak on the nose from Drew.

"What brings you back home?" his mom asked. "We're

overjoyed to see you, but work in Boston has always kept you so busy." Leticia's gaze was steely. He knew that she would have a host of questions for him. Nothing much got past her.

He shrugged, trying to downplay the situation. "Can we talk about that later? For now, I just want to revel in being back home. Where's Dad? And Theo?" he asked, looking around.

As if on cue, the kitchen door burst open to a gust of wind and the sight of his father and Theo standing there. Hudson braced himself for the worst. His relationship with his father had been frosty for the last three years. Missing his grandmother's funeral had been a bridge too far for his dad.

"Hud!" Twelve-year-old Theo practically exploded at the sight of his older brother. He didn't even bother taking off his snowy boots, which Hudson knew would cause a fuss with their mother. Theo threw himself against his chest and seemed to be hanging on for dear life. "I missed you," he cried out, his voice muffled.

Hud tousled his curly brown hair and said, "I missed you more." Truth was, his heart had been aching for a long time now due to his absence from his hometown. Although he had tried to make his life in Boston all about business and becoming successful, Serenity Peak had always pulled at his heartstrings.

"Jordy, say something," Hudson heard his mother say in a low voice to his father. A shuttered expression was stamped on Jordan Doherty's face. Hudson locked gazes with his father, unwilling to make a move until he knew that the man would meet him halfway. All of a sudden, the tension in the kitchen crackled with intensity.

"Son," his father said in a flat tone. "You're back. Why have you decided to grace us with your presence?"

Hudson sucked in a steadying breath. Being home was going to be more awkward than he'd imagined. For once in his life, Hud was tongue-tied. Why was it always so hard to talk to his father? Why hadn't they ever been close? To Hud it had always felt as if there had been a chasm between them ever since he'd chosen to go to college in Boston. It had only worsened when he had decided to make a life there.

His grandfather made a tutting sound and frowned at his son. "Jordy, give it a rest. Do I need to remind you of Ephesians 4:32?"

"No, you don't," Jordan snapped. "Forgiveness is a process. It can't be demanded or expected."

Ephesians 4:32 was Hud's favorite Bible verse. *And be ye kind one to another, tenderhearted, forgiving one another, even as God for Christ's sake hath forgiven you.*

"Hud, why don't you go to your room and switch up your clothes?" his mom suggested. As always she was trying her best to soothe a difficult situation. In this instance, she was trying to divert attention away from the tension between him and his father. She sent him a smile of encouragement. "If you want to rest up before lunch, that's fine. We'll be eating at noon time."

"Sounds good," Hudson said, heading back to the front hall to collect his luggage. His siblings trailed behind him, all of them offering their assistance. It felt nice to know that despite his father's coldness toward him he was still loved by certain family members. He hadn't been forgotten.

As he walked up the stairs toward his old bedroom, a part of him wondered if it still looked the same. His mother had always kept it the same throughout the years, but there was no telling what had happened over the course of three years. Frankly he wouldn't blame them if they'd turned it into a sewing room. Along the way, he stopped to admire a picture of his grandparents on their wedding day. He reached out and tapped his finger on his Nana's image. Hudson felt a pang in the region of his heart as he did so. Her very essence was in every nook and cranny of this house, yet she wasn't here anymore. And being confronted with this stark reality made him ache inside.

Rather than resting up, Hud hung out with his siblings, catching up on the goings-on in their lives and telling them about his life in Boston. He hadn't felt this relaxed in years. Or laughed as much as when Anna entertained them with knock-knock jokes and Theo shared fun facts about the solar system. Drew peppered him with questions about the Boston Celtics and the New England Patriots. Being with them made him feel as if no time at all had passed since he'd been here with them, even though Hud knew that wasn't true.

When it was lunchtime, they all gathered around the table in the dining room to share in the meal Leticia had prepared—Irish stew with green beans and sourdough bread. The aroma was so tantalizing it caused his stomach to grumble in anticipation. Things might have been almost perfect if his father didn't have a scowl on his face the entire meal.

All of a sudden at the end of the meal, a noisy banging on the front door rang out, catching them all by surprise.

"What in the world!" his mother exclaimed. "Who could that be? There's a closed sign up by the entrance." His family always closed up shop during meal times so they could break bread together without being interrupted. He couldn't recall a time when someone had ignored the sign.

"It sounds urgent," Bert said, his eyes wide. "I hope it isn't an emergency."

"Maybe someone really needs a Christmas tree," Anna suggested, giggling from behind her hand. Everyone laughed.

"I'll go see who's there," Theo offered, racing to open the door.

Low voices carried to the dining room, followed by the shuffling noise of feet making their way down the hall. Theo came charging into the room, his cheeks red with excitement. "We've got company," he announced with a flourish.

Hudson nearly spit his water out of his mouth at the sight of Molly standing in the entrance of his family's dining room. With her hands firmly planted on her hips, Molly's blue eyes glinted with fury. Her lips trembled.

"Hud, you caught me by surprise earlier."

A twisting sensation seized his gut. Molly was about to air him out in front of his whole family before he could tell them about the lawsuit. He hadn't imagined that she would beat a fast path over here so soon after they'd spoken.

Molly let out a huff of air. "I've had a few hours to think about the fact that you're suing me for co-ownership of Humbled." His family let out audible gasps. She took a few steps closer before jabbing her finger against his shoulder. "In case I didn't make it clear earlier, I'm prepared to fight you tooth and nail over this issue." She looked around the table at his family. "And I don't care who knows it."

Chapter Three

Molly stood in the Doherty's dining room fuming. She was a bit nervous about confronting Hud in front of his family, but that was one of the main reasons she'd shown up here. A niggling feeling in her gut had told her that the Doherty family knew nothing about Hud's lawsuit or his fanciful claims. Their reactions to her statement confirmed it!

Hud covered his face with his hands and let out a groan. "Couldn't this wait until later?"

She let out a snort. "Excuse me, but aren't you the person who showed up at my place of business before it had even opened for the day?" She folded her arms across her chest. "You didn't seem to be interested in waiting earlier. So let's lay it all on the table."

Hud rose from his seat and came face-to-face with her, only mere inches away. A vein was bouncing around by his eye. His hands were clenched by his sides.

"What's this all about? A lawsuit?" Leticia asked, her voice trembling. "Hudson?"

"Go ahead. Tell them," Molly instructed. She wasn't a vindictive person, but it felt good to turn things around on him if only for this one moment in time. Let him feel as caught off guard as she'd been earlier.

"I can't wait to hear this," Hud's father said, anger radiating from him in waves. "From the sounds of it, Hudson is barely back in town before he's stirring up trouble."

Tension crackled in the air like a roaring fire.

Suddenly she was full of regret for making an appearance at their home with such shocking news. The entire Doherty family appeared to be taken by surprise, much in the way she had been earlier this morning. The dynamic between Hud and his father was verging on explosive. Was she just as wrong as Hud had been by blindsiding her at her place of business?

"Molly, let's talk about this in private," Hud said in a low voice. He reached for her elbow, causing tremors to race along her arm.

Maybe he was right. Perhaps hashing this out in private could resolve things. If there was an opportunity to squash this lawsuit, then she would seize it.

"Talk about what?" Bert asked, his eyebrows knit together. "If it has to do with the shop, I want to hear what's being said. It meant a lot to Lillian."

Leticia reached over and patted Bert on the shoulder. "Don't get worked up. We don't need your blood pressure to go up."

Uh oh. Blood pressure? Making Bert sick hadn't been her intention in coming over to the Doherty home. She had been at work stewing over this until she'd felt steam coming out of her ears. Although Skye had tried to convince her not to go, she'd left the first chance she got, leaving the café in Estelle's care.

Hudson glared at Molly. She got the message loud and clear. If Bert's blood pressure shot up, it would be all her fault. Conveniently, Hud was forgetting that he'd been the one to throw the first jab. He could have talked to her before filing a lawsuit, but he'd chosen the low road. This wasn't something she ever would have anticipated in a million years.

She scowled right back at him. He wasn't going to intimidate her. Not even a little bit. Molly squared her shoulders and stood up as straight as she could.

It had always been like this between them, going all the way back to the sandbox. She didn't know if it had been a case of two strong-willed people going up against each other, but they had continually been at odds. Other than that brief period back in high school when they'd shown a romantic interest in one another. She shook off the memory as she'd done dozens of times before. That had been ages ago and Molly had put it in her rearview mirror. Their relationship had been sweet and meaningful, until she'd had the rug pulled out from underneath her. Hud had up and left Serenity Peak right after graduation without even saying goodbye.

Molly stuffed down the hurtful memory. After all, that was then and this was now. Their current situation wasn't going to be resolved by romanticizing their past. The only way to deal with a bully like Hud was to face him head on. At first she'd contemplated hiding herself away at Humbled, but that didn't make any sense to her. She was the injured party in the situation, not him. He was the one who'd walked away from Serenity Peak and turned his back on the town.

All of a sudden, a distinct rapping sound emanated from the front of the house.

"Is that another visitor?" Bert asked, looking perplexed.

"We sure are popular today," Theo said as he got up from his seat and headed down the hallway toward the front door. Within seconds, Abel Drummond was standing in the doorway, his presence immediately commanding attention. He was a bear of a man, tall and broad. As the owner of Sugar Works, a lucrative birch syrup company that hired a large number of townsfolk, Abel was well respected by all.

Jordan stood up from the table to greet him. "Abel," he said, grinning widely. "What brings you here? I haven't seen you in weeks."

Abel looked over at Hudson, then swung his gaze toward Molly. The way he looked at them told her that he knew all about the lawsuit.

"Skye called me and told me that Molly was on her way over here," Abel said. "She sounded quite upset about the situation between Hudson and Molly. Skye figured maybe I could help."

"What exactly is going on?" Leticia asked in an impatient tone. Clearly she was at her wit's end and wanted answers. "Hudson, what's all this about a lawsuit?"

Hud held his head up and locked gazes with his mother. "After much prayer and contemplation, I've decided to get back Nana's half of the shop."

A moment of silence ensued followed by a chorus of shouts.

"You did what?" Jordan asked. "Under what authority?" he roared.

Molly winced at the harsh tone infused in Jordan Doherty's voice. The way he spoke to Hud was over-the-top. As mad as she was with him, Molly hated the fact that Hud was on the receiving end of his dad's ire.

"If you remember, Nana made me the executor of her will, which means I have the authority," Hud said, his voice never wavering. "I'm protecting her interests." Even though he had missed the service, Hud had arranged the funeral along with his grandfather in the way she had envisioned.

As a simple woman with no large assets, settling her affairs had been straightforward.

"That's right," his grandfather chimed in. "Lillian wanted Hud to manage her affairs, and he handled everything nicely. Just as she wanted." Bert's voice was full of pride. She watched as Hud and his grandfather grinned at one another.

Once again, anger shot through Molly. This wasn't a trivial matter. Her whole life was hanging in the balance. She was on pins and needles just thinking about facing Hud in court. He was an educated man who worked with major companies in a big city.

"Hud, I can't believe you're really going through with this," Molly said, letting out a huff of air. She was becoming impatient, and she needed to get back to Humbled to relieve Estelle, who was manning the café all by herself.

Abel held up his hands. "If I may, I'd like to make a suggestion," Abel said, sounding calm and collected. "I've done my fair share of mediating issues here in town in an official capacity. I would like to help Molly and Hudson settle this issue without going to court."

Molly trusted Abel. He was a good man, honest and well loved in Serenity Peak.

Hud was listening to Abel as intensely as she was. Perhaps he would listen to the older man's wise counsel. If there was a reasonable solution, they both needed to embrace it.

"Perhaps we could convene in the den, just the three of us," Abel suggested. "How about it?"

"I'm fine with that," Molly said, yearning for a more private setting to discuss the matter. At the moment, Hud's younger siblings were being forced to listen to loud voices and accusations, which she feared could cause them to become upset. That was the last thing she wanted to happen. From what she knew of the Doherty family, they were fine people.

"Hudson? How about you?" Abel asked, focusing his gaze on him.

Appearing reluctant, Hud finally nodded and muttered something she couldn't quite hear. His demeanor wasn't promising, she realized. He was acting put out, as if he could barely stand to be alone with her and Abel. As Molly trailed behind Abel and Hud, she couldn't help but notice the concerned expression on Leticia's face. She sent her a smile, hoping to convey her intention to put this matter to rest before things spiraled out of control.

Once they were in the den, Molly sat down on a leather sofa while Hud took a spot on a comfy-looking love seat. Abel sat down beside her. Molly looked around the cozy room, admiring all the festive Christmas decorations. A small Christmas tree was in the corner, filled with glistening ornaments, candy canes and tinsel.

The heady smell of pine rose to her nostrils, serving as a reminder that Christmas was rapidly approaching. Even though it was weeks away, signs of the most blessed time of the year were all around them.

"I'm hoping that the two of you can come to an understanding before things take an ugly turn," Abel said.

"A little bit late for that," Molly murmured.

Hud swung his gaze in her direction. She cleared her throat. Somebody had to start the ball rolling. "With Christmas coming up, I really can't afford to be caught up in a legal battle instead of at my shop. The holiday season has proven to be the most lucrative for Humbled. It would really hurt my establishment."

"Well," Hud drawled, "if you agree to split the business with me, fifty-fifty, you won't have to worry about that."

Molly quirked her mouth. "And if I do that, I'll have a whole lot of other things to be worried about," she snapped. "No offense, but you're not exactly showcasing a trustworthy vibe."

Hud scoffed. "That's rich coming from someone whose family shut my Nana out of ownership of Humbled."

Molly jumped to her feet. "Take it back!" she shouted. "My family did nothing of the sort, and you know it."

Abel reached for her arm and gently pulled her back down to the sofa. "Both of you need to calm things down. I'm a mediator not a referee." Abel looked over at Hud, who was clenching his teeth so tightly she thought they might break.

"Hudson, I'd like to point out that we don't usually sue our neighbors here in Serenity Peak," Abel said, sounding stern. He ran his hand across his beard. "I understand that this is an issue you may feel passionate about, but there are other ways to resolve disputes than to make it a legal matter."

"Such as?" Hud asked, folding his arms across his chest.

Just then, there was a slight knock on the door before Hud's mother came in carrying a tray. "I don't want to interrupt, but I thought a nice cup of peppermint hot cocoa would benefit all of you."

"Much appreciated," Abel said as Leticia placed the tray down on the coffee table before leaving the room.

Hud picked up his mug and blew on it before carefully taking a sip. His mother knew how much he loved hot chocolate. He had a bad habit of burning his tongue on hot drinks due to his eagerness to taste them. The chocolate mixed with peppermint flavor delighted his taste buds. Hud had to stop himself from letting out a moan of appreciation. This wasn't the time or the place. Hud knew he had to keep his game face on.

"I hope you both know I'm a neutral party here. I've known both of you all your lives, as well as both of your families. My only agenda is in finding an amicable resolution," Abel explained. "First—" he turned to Hud "—I'd like to know when you plan to return to Boston."

Hud shrugged. "I've taken a leave of absence to deal with this situation, so there's no specific time frame," he explained.

Abel nodded. "Well, that's good to know. It helps."

"So, Abel, what exactly are you suggesting?" Hudson asked, raising his mug to his lips and taking a lengthy sip.

Abel stirred his own hot cocoa with a spoon, a thoughtful expression on his face.

"An amicable solution that will allow Molly to continue to conduct business during the lucrative holiday season." He cleared his throat. "I'm suggesting that it would be in the best interest of both parties if you could work together at Humbled for a period of thirty days. Hopefully, during that time you can find a way to sort through this mess."

"What?" Molly exploded. She sputtered as if her cocoa had gone down the wrong way. Abel leaned over, gently patting her on the back. "H-he hasn't even shown a shred of evidence that he has a legal leg to stand on."

Abel locked gazes with Hud. He had the strangest feeling that Abel knew a lot more about the situation than he was letting on.

"Molly, this isn't the first time this issue has been raised," Abel said, his tone somber.

"What are you talking about?" Molly asked. "I've never heard a whisper about any sort of dispute over the shop."

Abel nodded. "That's because it was squashed when Lillian and Bert raised it some years ago. As Christians, they chose not to hash it out in court."

"I remember discussing it with them at the time and being incredulous." Hud let out a snort. "And look what that got them. A whole lot of nothing!"

Abel shrugged. "Some might say it gave them peace."

"But not justice," Hud said. "He loveth righteousness and judgment: the earth is full of the goodness of the Lord. Psalm 33:5."

"If you want, we can go verse for verse," Molly quipped. "I've got a few up my sleeve as well."

"Let's not go there," Abel said, holding up his hands. Hud had the feeling that Abel was almost at his wit's end, which was saying something. Abel Drummond was known for his patience and understanding. He almost felt sorry for the man.

"Hudson, if I'm being honest, you know nothing about running Humbled," Abel said, focusing his gaze on him.

Hud nodded. "You're right, but the shop has been a part of my childhood thanks to Nana. It was a huge part of her life."

"If you're truly interested in co-ownership of the shop, then you should get some hands-on experience," Abel continued. "This would be a wonderful way to get acquainted with the business." He turned toward Molly. "Working with Hudson could really work to your benefit in many ways. Maybe you two will find a way to resolve this amicably."

"I'm not sure this could ever work out," she answered, her expression doubtful.

"Are you willing to give it a try in order to avoid a court case?" Abel pressed.

Molly bit her lip. "I—I guess so, as long as Hud agrees to stop this frivolous lawsuit."

He bit down on the inside of his cheek. "I wish you would stop calling it frivolous," he barked. "You're being insulting on purpose."

"And I wish you'd stayed in Beantown," Molly told him. "Far away from Serenity Peak."

Abel placed his head in his hands. "Lord, give me strength. Try to remember that we're heading into the most joyful and blessed season of all. Be kind to one another despite the friction. Do it for both of your grandmothers."

Whoa. Abel had just laid down the gauntlet, using their grandmothers as emotional blackmail. In that he was fighting for his Nana's legacy, Hud wasn't sure he should give much credence to what Abel was spouting. Time and again, he'd asked himself what Nana Lil would want him to do. Humbled had been a huge part of his childhood and he'd watched Lillian throw herself into the business with all of her heart and soul. She deserved to be remembered for her contributions. And as her grandson he felt a responsibility to act on her behalf. In the end, he'd decided to trust his gut and file the lawsuit.

But now, in the cold light of day, he had to be strategic. If he refused to try and mediate this issue, it could be held against him in court. Although he felt morally right in pursuing the case, he knew Molly had the upper hand. She had been running the establishment for many years and had transformed it into a showpiece. Adding a bookstore and modernizing the café had been a brilliant move, one he respected. Molly always had been highly motivated and intelligent.

He looked over at her. She was studying him as if he were a difficult subject that she simply couldn't grasp. Her beautiful blue eyes were full of questions. A part of him wanted to sit down with her, just the two of them, and talk things through. Like old times.

But, as he'd come to realize, those days were over. He was a lot more jaded in the here and now. Nana's death had gutted him. He'd lost a part of himself that he could never get back. He still ached over the fact that she had unexpectedly passed away when he was on his way to the airport. Shame at not having been at her side had kept him from attending her funeral.

"So, Hudson, what will it be?" Abel asked, looking at him expectantly. Molly looked as if she was holding her breath waiting for his answer. He felt a pang of guilt upon noticing the signs of tension stamped on her pretty face. Molly looked scared, and he truly hated making her feel that way. He knew quite well what it felt like to have the bottom fall out of your world.

He sucked in a steadying breath. Abel had backed him into a corner, one he couldn't find a way out of. The wheels were beginning to turn around in his head. Maybe sticking around town and running Humbled with Molly might work to his advantage.

"Thirty days means I'll have to stay for Christmas, right?" he asked. Although Christmas had been his favorite time of year as a child, the older he became the less entranced he was by all the trappings of the holiday season. But he imagined his siblings would get a kick out of spending time with him and enjoying all the festive aspects of the season.

"Yes," Molly answered. "It's the busiest time of year at Humbled. The Christmas season isn't just about profit for us. We try to give back to the community and inspire hope." Her voice cracked, and she stopped for a moment to collect herself. "So, Hud, I would suggest that you turn that frown upside down if you plan to work at Humbled."

How had he forgotten the way Molly had always been Miss Bossy Pants. That had been her nickname back in grade school. The memory made him chuckle. She'd hated the fact that the boys had called her that. Every single time her cheeks had reddened.

"This isn't a joke," Molly scolded, her lips pursed.

"I know that," he answered, looking her straight in the eye. "I'm treating this with the utmost reverence."

And he really was. In addition to getting justice for his grandmother, this entire situation could be very profitable for him and his family. Humbled was situated on Main Street in downtown Serenity Peak. Due to Sugar Works, tourism had blossomed in the small town. Property values were up, especially in the area where Humbled was located. Had the situation with the shop been handled differently, his grandparents would have benefited as they'd grown older.

"Is this something you can live with?" Abel asked him. "I know it might be difficult to take time away from your life in Boston. And I know you're quite successful at what you do." A huge grin overtook his face. "Your mama is quite proud of your achievements."

Hud's throat tightened. His mother always told him how proud she was of his strong work ethic and how he carved out a life for himself so far away from Alaska. She believed in him, much like his grandmother had. He swallowed past the lump in his throat. At random moments like this one, the loss of his Nana tugged at him, threatening to pull him under.

He'd set this all in motion without thinking things through. Perhaps this time at the café would allow him to finesse the situation and explain everything to his family.

If he flatly refused Abel's suggestion, it wouldn't look good for him. Tongues would wag in Serenity Peak. He didn't want to get off on the wrong foot.

"I can work something out so that it won't be a problem," he said. "I need a day to get settled here, but I can report to the shop day after tomorrow," Hudson said.

"Does that work for you, Molly?" Abel asked.

She waited a moment as if she were thinking it over. She then nodded. "Yes, it's fine," she answered. "I'll find a way to make it work. I'm a professional."

Abel heaved a sigh of relief. "Hallelujah!" he said, clapping. "This is the way a community works to resolve conflicts. I'm proud of you both."

Molly stood up and hugged Abel. "Thanks for helping out," she told him. "I appreciate it."

She turned toward Hudson and held out her hand. "Let's call a truce for the next thirty days," she said. "Agreed?"

Hudson reached out and shook. "Agreed," he said. As soon as he made contact, he felt a pulsing sensation in his fingers and palm. He was so surprised by the unexpected current between them that he quickly let go of her. Molly's eyes widened at the contact. Whatever that was, she'd felt it too. He wasn't imagining things.

"I've got to go," Molly said, quickly putting on her parka and heading toward the door.

"I should get back to it myself," Abel said. "I'll walk you out, Molly. See you soon, Hudson."

"Bye," Hudson said in a low voice. He was feeling a bit overwhelmed by the whirlwind events of his first day back in town. Once the door closed behind them, his mind began to race with questions. Had he been outsmarted by Abel? Had he been swayed by the mention of his grandmother?

The thought of working side by side with Molly at Humbled was a bit disorienting. Just a few hours ago, she hadn't even wanted him in the shop, yet now she would have to welcome him with open arms. He imagined that Molly was also reeling from this unexpected turn of events.

He had almost laughed out loud when Abel mentioned his important job and work schedule. The truth was, he had nothing to go back to in Boston. If he thought about his situation for too long, he might never get up out of this chair. Life in Beantown hadn't ever lived up to his expectations.

In many ways, Humbled was a lifeline for him, one that he couldn't afford to let go of. Perhaps if he could make this work his family would view him in a positive light. Molly might think that the next thirty days was a win for her, but in reality it was just a reprieve from the inevitable. He wasn't giving up. Not without a fight.

Chapter Four

Molly finished the workday at Humbled in a semi-daze, her mind occupied by thoughts of Hud and their face-off at his family's house. Her cheeks warmed at the memory of how she'd interrupted the Doherty's meal and confronted him. Making such a scene wasn't like her at all. She was a fairly reserved person who didn't like to raise her voice. But she'd been motivated by a righteous anger. Tensions had been running high between them, but thanks to Abel, the situation had quieted down. They had reached a compromise that would keep the matter out of court. *For now*, she thought.

She should be happy, but she wasn't! A nauseous feeling swept over her at the realization that thirty days wasn't very long to make peace with someone. Bless Abel for believing it could happen and for being such a skilled mediator.

Hud had come back to town like a wrecking ball, intent on stirring things up. He'd always been the kid to stir the pot. Clearly he hadn't changed one bit, she fumed. Now she was stuck working in close confines with him at the shop. This time of year was supposed to be filled with eggnog and evergreens, peppermint lattes and goodwill toward mankind.

She couldn't help but worry that Hudson Doherty was going to ruin Christmas.

Deep in thought, Molly locked up the shop for the evening and said her goodbyes to Vinny and Estelle. Earlier she'd clued them in to the situation with Hud, letting them know that he would be working with them for the next month. They had both been shocked at the turn of events, immediately asking if their jobs would be in jeopardy. Molly had told them that they both had job security and she had no intention of letting either of them go.

Even though she lived above the shop, Molly couldn't go upstairs and unwind just yet. She had an important errand to run that involved checking in on her grandfather, Phineas. He had been floundering a bit since the death of her grandmother, Eva. He lived next door to her parents, who were out of town until next week. Since both of her sisters, Janine and Casey, had moved away from Serenity Peak after getting married, the responsibility of checking on her grandfather had been placed on her shoulders.

Not that she minded spending time with Pops. He was the best person she had ever known. Making a fuss over him from time to time made him feel good.

For the entire ride over to his property, she cranked up holiday tunes on the radio, intent on pretending as if the events of today hadn't happened. She got a little choked up when her gran's favorite Christmas song—"Carol of the Bells"—blared from the speakers.

As she drove up to the house and then stepped out of her vehicle, Molly couldn't help but notice that there were no holiday adornments anywhere to be found. Normally, her grandfather had the place ablaze with Christmas lights and lawn decorations. Even right after Gran's death, he'd made sure to decorate the place with all the bells and whistles of the holiday season.

Why hadn't she noticed this a few days ago when she'd popped by? She fretted that perhaps he hadn't had anyone to help him, with her parents away and her busy work schedule.

After a slight knock on the front door, Molly let herself into the home. "Pops, it's me," she called out, waiting for a reply.

Seconds later, she heard his raspy voice. "I'm in the kitchen fixing dinner."

A heady aroma filled the air, reminding Molly of countless meals she'd enjoyed at her grandparents' table. She followed the scent, walking down the hall toward the kitchen. As soon as she crossed the threshold, her grandpa came into view. He was standing at the stove stirring a pot with one hand while leaning on a cane with the other.

"Pop," she said, quickly making her way to his side. "I thought you weren't supposed to be cooking."

He let out a groan. "Now don't you start with me. I've been making my meals for most of my life," he grumbled. "Your mom made some meals for me before she left and put them in my freezer. Bless her heart, but she skimps on the salt."

Molly let out a chuckle. She pressed a kiss on his cheek. "Maybe because your doctor wants you to watch your sodium."

He rolled his eyes and kept stirring. "God has seen fit to keep me around for almost eighty-two years. I consider myself blessed beyond measure. I'm not going to let arthritis or my blood pressure rule my life."

This wasn't the first time he'd balked at a doctor's order. His arthritis had become a major health concern, affecting his gait and his coordination. Still and all, Phineas rejected all attempts to limit his activities. Molly couldn't really blame him. He wanted to cherish the remaining days he had left.

"Is that stew I smell?" she asked, veering away from the touchy subject. She knew Pops well enough to realize that he wasn't going to give an inch. Better to spend quality time with him that didn't involve butting heads.

"It is," he said. "Your gran's recipe. I think I've almost got it replicated, although it'll never taste exactly like hers."

Molly heard the plaintive note in his voice. Even though Gran had been gone for three years now, Molly still saw sadness emanating from his chocolate brown eyes. She'd come to realize that grief was a never-ending journey. He would mourn his wife for the rest of his life. She, along with the rest of her family, would have to continue to shower him with affection so he knew he was loved.

Pops turned off the burner. "Why don't you set the table for us? I have a bowl of salad in the fridge and a loaf of sourdough bread that I baked earlier."

"You sure know the way to a girl's heart," Molly teased. She enjoyed an easy rapport with her grandfather. He was a big bear of a man, who looked way more intimidating than he actually was. Phineas had a gruff facade, but he was gooey marshmallow at his center.

Phineas grinned as he placed the stew on the table then went toward the cupboard for plates, bowls and utensils. Molly busied herself with the salad and cutting generous slices of bread. They ate in companionable silence as they enjoyed the hearty meal. With every bite, Molly asked herself how she was going to break the news to him about Hud's return and the potential lawsuit.

"What's with the furrowed brow?" he asked as he pushed

his empty plate away from him. "I can always tell when you're fretting about something."

Molly wiped her mouth with her napkin and placed it down on her plate.

She hated to be the bearer of bad news, but there was no point in hiding this information from him. He had grown up in this town, and he knew just about everyone. It was best for Molly to be the one to tell Pops since gossip flew on the wind in Serenity Peak. She didn't want him to get blindsided.

She cleared her throat. "Today was a bit stressful," she told him, biting her lip. "I had an early morning visitor at Humbled." Molly sat back in her chair and folded her arms across her chest. "An unwelcome one."

His eyebrows rose. "Who was it?"

"Hudson Doherty. He served me with legal papers for ownership of Humbled." She pushed the words out of her mouth before she could chicken out.

Pops's features went slack. "You've got to be kidding me."

"I wish I were," Molly said, shaking her head. "For the life of me, I can't figure out why he's doing this." She quickly filled him in on the meeting at the Doherty's home and Abel's skillful intervention.

"Bless Abel," Pops said. "He's a good man. Always has been."

"The very best," Molly agreed. "The upside is the lawsuit is on hold, but the downside is that I'm stuck working with Hud for a solid month."

Phineas scowled. "I don't like to talk ill of folks, but Hudson was always a bit of a ne'er do well. Always thinking only of himself." He let out a snort. "What do they call those folks? Narcissists?"

"You're preaching to the choir." Molly said. All of a sudden she felt deflated. "I don't even know what to do or how to move forward. I love Humbled and being a shop owner." She let out a sob. "The thought of losing the business is unbearable."

Phineas leaned across the table and thumped his palm down. "Humbled was your gran's pride and joy. Her creation from conception to construction. You're going to dig in your heels and fight, Molly," he urged. "And you won't be alone either. The entire Truitt family will have your back. We're not just going to hand over your gran's legacy to anyone, least of all Hudson Doherty."

The next morning, Hud dragged himself out of bed. Despite the temptation to burrow under the covers, he wasn't about to oversleep and run the risk of being late to work. If that happened, Molly would never let him live it down. Although they'd both agreed to work together through the holidays, Molly had been visibly unhappy about the arrangement. So much for being the bigger person. Maybe he shouldn't have relented so quickly. This work situation would be awkward.

Of course he was the bad guy. Even his own father had expressed displeasure over his actions regarding Humbled. He'd shrugged it off. Knowing that he was doing all of this for his grandmother made it all worth it. The ache of missing her caused his chest to feel tight. They had always been so close. She'd been the one who had insisted that he travel all the way to Boston to attend college.

"The East Coast has the best universities, so that's where you should be." Her words echoed in his ears. No one had ever believed in his potential as much as she had.

As he sat on the edge of his bed, he heard a slight creaking noise as his door slowly opened. Theo stuck his head in and grinned at him.

"I just wanted to make sure that you were really here and that I wasn't dreaming," his little brother said as he entered the room and sat down next to him.

Hudson tousled his brother's curls. "Of course I'm here. Back where I belong," he said, winking. Saying the words out loud surprised him since this particular realization had been a long time coming. He'd wasted so many years trying to distance himself from his hometown, choosing to focus instead on his career and life in a big city. He was discovering that nothing suited him as well as Alaska.

"Well, Mom made griddle cakes with homemade syrup, scrambled eggs and sausage for breakfast," Theo told him. "You better come down before Drew eats it all."

Hud chuckled as he watched Theo beat a fast path out of his room.

His stomach grumbled in appreciation. It had been almost four years since he'd tasted his mother's griddle cakes. He couldn't put into words how much he'd missed the smells and sounds of the Doherty household. He quickly got dressed then went downstairs.

"Morning, Hudson," his mother greeted him. "Sit down before the food gets cold."

"I'm going to have to eat quickly," he said, glancing at his watch. "It's almost time to head out." A plate full of deliciousness was placed down in front of him, and he didn't hesitate to dig in.

"Look at you," Leticia said, giving him an approving nod. "Be careful. You're going to turn a lot of girls' heads in town."

Theo let out a groan and slapped his hand to his forehead.

Hudson looked down at his jacket and slacks. Although

he might be overdressed for Humbled, it was important to make a good impression on one's first day at work. Many of the townsfolk hadn't seen him in quite some time. He wanted to make them stand up and take notice. It surprised him that he wanted validation from the Serenity Peak community. For so long he'd told himself that he was past caring about the opinions of others. Being dyslexic had given him a lot of insecurity in his younger years. Looking back, it had been one of the reasons he'd wanted to go to Boston and get his degree. School had always been a struggle, and he'd been looking for a fresh start.

Ten minutes later he was in the driver's seat and making his way to town. Festive holiday touches were everywhere on Main Street. Christmas had always been the most wonderful time of the year in Serenity Peak, and he imagined nothing had changed in that regard. He parked the rental in the lot behind Humbled and decided to take a quick stroll to check out store windows. He paused in front of The Toy Box, the local toy store that had been around since before he was born. The establishment had always been his favorite as a child. The window display made him smile. Toy trains dusted with fake snow. A ballerina dressed in pink tulle. A huge teddy bear with a bright red bow. He continued walking along the street, looking through all of the display windows and soaking in the holiday flair. Even the barbershop had oversize candy canes and nutcrackers on display.

Hud arrived at Humbled a few minutes before seven. Feeling upbeat, he began whistling a happy tune as he stepped inside the shop. Lights were blazing from within, even though he was a little early. Leave it to Molly to one-up him by arriving first. She had always been a bit of a type A, even as a kid. He clenched his teeth at the idea of taking his marching orders from Molly. They were going to clash like oil and water.

Think positive. This is all for Nana's legacy.

His footsteps rang out on the hardwood floor, making a little bit of a clatter. He heard a rustling sound, followed by Molly appearing from behind the bakery display case. She had been bent down so low filling the case with baked goods that he hadn't seen her.

"Morning, Molly," he said, nodding his head at her.

"Why are you wearing a suit?" Molly asked, gaping at him. So much for pleasantries.

Leave it to Molly to make him feel foolish within mere moments.

"This is how I dress for work," he said. "Is there a problem?" Way to make him feel uncomfortable on his first day.

She twisted her mouth. "This isn't Wall Street," she said. Molly shook her head, making a disapproving sound. "You're either going to be working in the bookstore or right here at the café. In both places you'll be rolling up your sleeves and being hands-on. There are days when I leave here covered in crumbs, flour and espresso."

"Point taken," he said, gritting his teeth. He should have known, but old habits died hard. The workforce he was entering was worlds apart from anything he'd known in Boston.

She came out from behind the counter and stood face-to-face with him. "Since you'll be working here, you're going to have to know the lay of the land."

"A tour would be nice," Hudson said. He looked around the place. Humbled wasn't big, but what it lacked in size, it made up for in charm and coziness. From what he could see, it was a great spot. He totally understood why it had become so popular.

"Right this way," Molly said. So far her tone was crisp. No one would ever suspect that they'd grown up together and had once enjoyed a brief romance. Not that he could blame her for being a bit salty. He'd come back to town and blindsided her. "Let's start in the bookstore," she suggested. "Do you know how to work a cash register?"

"It's been a while, but I'm sure it'll all come back to me. I worked at a deli during my college years," he explained.

"Well, we also process credit card payments. I can give you a quick refresher course if you need it."

"Good to know," Hudson said. "I think I'll take you up on that."

There was no door between the shops, simply an open doorway, creating an intimate vibe and a nice flow throughout the establishment.

A smile tugged at his lips as they crossed the threshold into the bookstore. His grandmother had adored books of all genres—romance, Shakespeare, memoirs, mysteries. This shop was infused with her sensibilities. Brightly colored shelves brimming with books. Little nooks and crannies where customers could sit down and curl up with a story. On his quick walk around the store, Hudson spotted dozens of familiar titles.

Nana was etched in the very foundation of Humbled. Just standing in this space reminded him of everything he was fighting for. Legacy. Acknowledgment. Affirmation.

Most of all, Hudson could feel his grandmother here, as if she were a part of the walls and foundation. So many times he'd wanted to feel her presence—had prayed about it—but up until now he hadn't. A poignant memory caused his chest to tighten. Nana had spent so many hours here stocking the shelves and taking pains to make sure the place appeared tidy and appealing. She would sit Hud on her knee and read his favorite books to him. There had even been a little nook for him to nap in if he became sleepy.

Hudson looked at the space behind the register. A beautiful framed picture of Molly's grandmother, Eva, hung on the wall. A slow irritation began to burn inside of him. His Nana's photo should be hanging right alongside hers. She'd done so much to earn a place of honor here.

"Hud! Did you hear me?" Molly asked.

Her voice snapped him out of his thoughts. This place evoked such strong memories of Nana that he'd been in a daze. He'd almost forgotten Molly was here. "Sorry. What did you say?"

"I said it might be a good time to look over today's specials and familiarize yourself with the café. That's where you'll be working today."

The café! He wasn't going to admit it, but he didn't know a lot about specialty drinks or baked goods. Hudson took his own coffee black with no sugar or cream. He'd never been one to order fancy drinks with whipped cream and syrups. Thankfully, he considered himself a fast learner.

As she led him back toward the café, he swept his gaze over the area. The place had come a long way since he'd last lived in Serenity Peak. Molly had really turned it into a showpiece, which made him think the establishment must be profitable. Modernizing the shop couldn't have been cheap. Pastel hues dominated the space—pink, baby blue, rose and cream. A twinkling chandelier hung above the counter. An elaborate mural featuring cherubs had been painted on the walls. There were intimate tables for two and larger ones that accommodated more customers. Something for everyone.

Humbled had a serene ambiance. No doubt it appealed to folks looking for a morning pick me up, a good book to read or a fun spot to hang out with friends. The place had so much potential. He wondered if Molly was maximizing all the possibilities. Suddenly all his marketing skills came alive. So many ideas were zooming around in his brain, just waiting to be introduced. The shop could benefit by having fun events that would draw in a wider clientele. Social media could be utilized to boost in-house promotions on drinks, baked goods and books.

"Are mornings busy here?" he asked. Hudson hadn't stuck around long enough yesterday to make any sort of assessment.

"Mornings are the busiest time of day at Humbled." She let out a chuckle. "Buckle up, hotshot," she said, smirking at him. "You wanted to be in the café-bookstore business, so consider the next three hours your audition."

Chapter Five

Hud wiped his arm across his brow and let out a beleaguered sigh. Molly hadn't exaggerated one bit about the morning rush. Honestly, he didn't know if he was coming or going. He was pretty rusty at the cash register, so he'd been tasked with taking orders and delivering items to customers at their tables. Hudson had made quite a few errors, to the point where his actions resembled something from a Three Stooges movie.

He kept confusing the gingerbread latte with the pumpkin swirl frappé. And he couldn't keep the pastries straight. Chocolate croissants. Cheese Danish. Rugelah. Scones. His brain was beginning to feel a little bit scrambled. Sometimes he became confused with words due to his dyslexia, even though he'd developed techniques over the years that helped him out.

"Hudson Doherty! Is that you?" An older woman with silver hair stepped up to the counter and leaned over it, peering at him through her spectacles.

"Mrs. Gates," he said, quickly recognizing his childhood piano teacher.

"You look different, Hudson. You've grown into a very distinguished young man," she said with an approving nod. "Boston looks good on you."

"Why thank you," he said, standing taller in his suit due to her compliment.

"I'd like a plain croissant and a coffee with sugar and a splash of peppermint creamer." She winked at him. "And you have an open invitation to come to lunch at my place. I'd love to catch up."

"Coming right up. I'd be honored," Hudson said, grinning. He was grateful for an easy order and a friendly face. So far his reception in Serenity Peak had been mixed, with half of the folks acting as if he were an alien from another planet while the rest had been welcoming.

He felt Molly's eyes on him as he plated the croissant and filled a mug with coffee. Some instinct told him that she wanted and expected him to fall on his face. He wasn't going to give her the satisfaction. Hudson was determined to learn all the ins and outs of Humbled and become fantastic at his new job. He couldn't afford to give Molly any ammunition against him, especially if he ended up moving forward with the lawsuit. As things stood, it could go either way.

"Had enough yet?" Molly asked. "I know this isn't what you're used to."

What did she know about his life in Boston? If nothing else, he had always been a hard worker. Being dyslexic, he'd had to work harder to succeed academically.

He plastered the biggest, widest grin on his face. "Of course not. I'm beginning to get the swing of things," he said. "I couldn't be happier."

"Good to know," she said. "We just got an order for six eggnog frappés. It would be great if you could take care of that."

He felt his eyes widening. "You want *me* to make the drinks?"

"Is that too much for you?" Molly asked, her brow raised. He just knew she was relishing the fact that he was in over his head. His crash course in making drinks before the café opened had been short and sweet. It hadn't adequately prepared him for the onslaught of orders and the varieties. Molly had given him a cheat sheet on how to make each drink, but to Hudson it still felt like climbing a mountain in bare feet.

"Of course not," he said. "I've got this!"

Molly shot him a look of grudging respect. "Awesome. Estelle's tied up in the bookstore going over our inventory. Vinny won't be in until after lunchtime. And I've got my hands full with the rest of the customers."

"No worries," Hudson said. "Let me go knock out this order."

He pushed past the swinging door leading to the kitchen and headed over to the counter. He shrugged off his jacket and pulled off his tie before rolling up the sleeves of his shirt. Several state-of-the-art blenders sat in front of him. He'd instantly recognized the brand since his ex-girlfriend, Lana, had owned one and sworn by the product. Molly must have been going for a theme since the blenders were also shades of pastel.

He clutched his recipe cheat in his hand and went down the list of ingredients he needed.

"Okay, this isn't too bad," he said, reading the list out loud. "Milk. Sugar. Coffee. Ice. Syrup. And top it off with nutmeg and whipped cream." He rooted around the counter for all of his ingredients, eager to get this order completed.

Then he dived right in, placing all of the main ingredients into the blender and adding ice. He turned the blender on and hit the pulse button. The machine made a loud clatter that echoed throughout the kitchen. The heady smell of eggnog reached his nostrils. Once the consistency seemed right, Hudson turned off the machine. Feeling proud of himself, he poured the liquid into six tall glasses, spraying liberal amounts of whipped cream on top before sprinkling them with nutmeg.

"This is what's called crushing it," he said as he walked past Molly at the counter.

"Congrats," she said dryly. "The table by the first window is eagerly awaiting their order."

With his head held high, Hudson carried the tray filled with drinks over to the customers. He wondered if they were tourists since he didn't recognize any of them. Thanks to Sugar Works, Humbled had benefited from the influx of visitors to Serenity Peak. He didn't know if Molly had a gameplan, but it would be smart to try and further capitalize on tourism dollars.

"Eggnog frappés are served," he said, placing the drinks on the table while balancing the tray. He wobbled a little bit but managed to keep the platter steady.

A little girl with red pigtails wiggled with excitement in her seat. "Oh, I can't wait," she squealed. "My favorite."

"They look delicious," the man with the beard said.

Everyone oohed and aahed as he handed out straws and excused himself. Hudson practically strutted back to the counter. Making a batch of eggnog frappés felt like a huge win, one that he seriously needed right now. More than anything, he wanted to prove that he belonged here at Humbled just as much as Molly. If he had to whip up eggnog frappés to prove his worth, then that was what he would do!

"Houston. I think we have a problem," Molly said, jutting her chin in the direction of his customers. Hudson had a sinking feeling in the pit of his stomach as he watched the table of six reacting badly to his frappés.

A groan slipped past his lips as he quickly walked back to the table.

"Is there a problem?" he asked. Judging by the looks on their faces, they weren't enjoying themselves.

The child scrunched up her nose and made a face. "This tastes awful."

"Mattie, mind your manners," her mother scolded. She looked up at Hudson. "I'm sorry but something is a bit... off with the drinks."

"Oh," he said, instantly feeling deflated. "I'm so sorry. I can't imagine why."

But of course he could. He wasn't an experienced barista or baker. Even though the drink had seemed uncomplicated, clearly he'd made a misstep. Now he would have to do a walk of shame back to the counter.

"My apologies," he said. "I'll be right back with a better version," he promised.

He cleared the table, and when he headed back to the kitchen Molly was waiting for him there.

"Don't say a word," he said, placing the tray on the counter. The last thing he needed was her judgment. "Clearly these aren't fit for human consumption." One by one he began to toss the contents of each glass in the sink.

"Yeah, I figured that was the case when I saw your ingredients," Molly said, her lips twitching with mirth. He didn't even have time to process how good she looked when she smiled.

He frowned. "What do you mean? I used a classic recipe. Zero frills," he explained.

Molly reached for the canister of ground coffee and held it up in the air. "Did you use this to make the drinks?"

"Of course I did," he said. "Shouldn't I have?"

"It's not instant coffee. It's chili powder," Molly told

him. At this point she was clearly trying not to burst into laughter. She was biting down on her lip and avoiding eye contact.

"Chili powder," he said, grimacing. "Why was chili powder on the counter?"

"Because it's used in several of the pastries. In moderation," she said, raising her hand to cover her mouth.

"So I basically just served up chili frappés." No wonder his customers had hated the drinks. Hudson slapped his hand on his forehead. Talk about a rookie mistake. Sometimes this happened due to his dyslexia when he was rushing to perform a task.

All of sudden he heard a snorting noise emanating from Molly. She was hiding her face behind her hand and trying to keep it together. A hoot of laughter erupted from inside of her, almost as if against her will. Within seconds she was full-on laughing out loud with tears streaming down her cheeks.

"I—I'm sorry, Hud. I really shouldn't be laughing, but—" She erupted into another fit of giggles.

"You're all heart, Molly," Hud said, turning toward the counter and searching for the tin of coffee so that he could remake the frappés.

Molly might think he was a joke, but as a dyslexic these mistakes sometimes happened. In addition, he had been diagnosed with ADHD at eighteen, which had only come about thanks to Nana pushing for him to get tested. Her belief in Hud and his potential had been awe inspiring. It was just one of the many reasons he was now fighting for her.

Clearly Molly had forgotten a signature trait of his. Ever since childhood, he had been extremely driven. He'd never been one to give up easily. He had come back home to fight for his grandmother's share of Humbled and, in doing so, make her proud. Hudson wasn't going to let one embarrassing moment stop him from pressing forward.

If anything, the echo of Molly's laughter ringing in his ears served as a huge incentive. Failure wasn't an option.

Molly didn't like feeling badly for Hud, but at the moment she did. After the way he'd shown up and thrown down the gauntlet by serving her with legal papers, she didn't feel that she owed him a single thing. He was way too cocky for his own good. Not to mention that he was totally wrong about his grandmother being a cofounder of Humbled. It absolutely made no sense. As long as she could remember, the shop had been her gran's vision come to fruition.

Compassion doesn't cost you a thing.

Her gran's voice buzzed in her ears, reminding her that kindness was free.

She hadn't meant to hurt Hud's feelings by laughing at him. It hadn't been malicious. She had a serious funny bone at times, and it had been tickled by Hud's snafu with the ingredients. The crestfallen expression on his face—devoid of any arrogance or bravado—had touched her. And a memory had been triggered of him having dyslexia. She didn't know if that was the root cause of the error, but she felt incredibly guilty for making light of his discomfort.

Seeing Hud so humbled had swept Molly back in time to when they had gotten close and bonded romantically after a few months of dating. That version of Hud had been tender and sweet. She'd seen a side of him that had been hidden away during their younger years. And then he'd taken off for college, leaving her confused and a bit jaded.

She headed back to the café floor, leaving Hud to recreate the drinks without her standing nearby. As she usually did when a mix-up occurred with customers, Molly took some pastries from the case and placed them on a large plate. She walked over to the Dennison family, greeting them with a large smile. "Compliments of Humbled. Enjoy these baked goods while you wait for the frappés."

She continued to smile as they showered her with thanks and dug into the pastries.

A little line had formed at the checkout area, so Molly quickly walked over to handle those customers. "Sorry for the wait," she said, noticing her friend, Destiny, was next in line.

"Destiny! I almost didn't recognize you. Loving the new look."

Destiny greeted her with a huge grin, making her pretty face even more radiant. She patted her hair, which was now styled in a chic bob. "I decided to do something a little different for the holidays."

"I approve," she said, reaching for Destiny's credit card and processing her order.

"Was that... Hud I just saw?" Destiny asked, her voice lowered.

Molly nodded. "It sure was. It's a long story, but he'll be working here through the holidays." This was just the beginning of the questions. Hud's return, combined with him working at Humbled, would be fodder for lots of town talk.

Her friend's eyes bulged. "That must be one complex story, one that I'd love to hear over lunch. It's been too long."

"Let's get something on the books soon," Molly said, handing Destiny her credit card and receipt. Molly watched her friend exit the shop. Destiny owned a successful K-9 service training business where she helped a lot of struggling people. She had recently gotten married to Luke

Adams, one of their childhood buddies, who'd been a client of hers. Seeing the two of them together made Molly feel a mixture of happiness and envy. She felt the same way about Skye and Ryan. Clearly, she was yearning for a love of her own.

Both times she'd managed to open herself up to a romantic partner, everything had blown up in her face. She didn't think that she had the strength to put herself out there again. Hud had run away from their budding relationship while Will had made promises he just hadn't kept. Will had ended things abruptly after telling her he was so serious about her that he had been looking at engagement rings. She had been blindsided by both men. And left without answers. Had she done something to cause Will to change his mind about marrying her?

She wanted what Skye had with Ryan. Sadly, she couldn't picture it happening. Not to mention that so much of her life was now tied up in running Humbled.

Lately, she'd begun to wonder if she was blocking some of the blessings offered in her community. She no longer sang with the women's choir at Serenity Church. She couldn't think of the last time she had been out on a date or even met someone new. Being so devoted to Humbled had limited her ability to connect with others in meaningful ways. Of course she saw a lot of townsfolk while working, but those interactions were fleeting at best. Although she baked with love in her heart it wasn't the same as connecting with people.

Hud walked past her carrying a tray of six frappés. He was making his way toward the Dennisons. She could hear the low rumble of conversation but not what they were saying. She watched as they tasted the drinks and nodded their heads enthusiastically. Molly released the breath she'd been holding and focused on her next order. A few moments later, she headed toward the kitchen in search of some creamer for iced coffees.

While she had her head buried in the fridge, the kitchen door swung open, and out of the corner of her eye, she saw Hud enter.

Molly turned toward him. "Nice save out there, Hud. I know this is all new to you, so your efforts are appreciated."

Hud's mouth opened, and he gaped at her. "Th-thanks. They seem really pleased with the do-over."

"That's what we like," Molly said, sounding chirpy. "Happy customers means repeat customers. Good job," she added, feeling like a peppy cheerleader. This being kind thing wasn't as easy as Gran had always told her. Interacting with Hud was still a bit awkward. Molly didn't want to be mean, but she couldn't pretend as if Hud wasn't trying to steal her family's business out from under her.

He arched an eyebrow. "You're being suspiciously nice," he told her. "What's up with that?"

"I'm a nice person," Molly quipped, "even to Bostonians who try to sue me."

Hud puffed out his chest. "I'm Alaskan born and bred," he said, winking. "Boston was never my home."

"So you'd really give up your life in the big city to run this shop?" she asked. Molly was genuinely curious about his answer.

"I would," he said. "In a heartbeat."

She allowed that tidbit to settle over her for a moment. From the sounds of it, Hud was looking to reestablish his Alaskan roots.

Molly narrowed her gaze as she looked at him. As always, Hud was a hard person to figure out. At moments like this one, she totally believed he was being sincere. Her gut twisted as she remembered how he'd disillusioned her once before. She'd believed in him until there'd been nothing left to believe in. Their relationship hadn't lasted long, but she'd always thought that she deserved a lot more from Hud than being ghosted.

It wouldn't be shocking if he up and left town again without a word of explanation. After all, he'd done it once before. The past was a powerful predictor of future behavior. She wouldn't be the least bit surprised.

"What took place earlier with the frappés…that happens all the time when you're running a bakery and trying to find your footing," Molly said. "There's a steep learning curve."

His mouth twisted. "That you don't think I can successfully navigate, right?"

She shook her head. "I'm not saying that. What I am saying is that running a business isn't easy, and it comes with ups and downs."

"I appreciate the heads-up, Molly. I really do," he said.

She let out the breath she'd been holding. Hud had never been one to listen to advice even if it was well intentioned. Maybe working alongside Hud wasn't going to be as difficult as she had imagined. He was being cordial and seemed to be listening to what she had to say. For a moment there, she'd thought he was going to be difficult.

"Maybe you should rethink this whole thing, Hud," she said softly. "I understand that you might believe my family took something from yours, but that's not the case at all. Being here and working at Humbled would just be spinning your wheels. In the end it won't change a thing."

Hud blinked a few times, once again drawing her attention to his extraordinary hazel eyes. They held and locked with her own. A certain tension hovered in the space between them.

She noticed a sudden shift in him. Hud's mouth formed a hard line, and his eyes seemed to darken from hazel to brown. Perhaps she shouldn't have been so blunt. Maybe this wasn't the right time or place for this discussion.

He leaned in toward her so that their faces were mere inches away from one another. So close she noticed the tiny scar above his lip, the one he'd gotten sledding down the biggest hill in town when they were small.

"Molly, if you think I'm giving up on Humbled, you've got another think coming." He shrugged. "I suggest that you buckle up, because I'm here for the long haul."

Chapter Six

The tension was so thick inside Humbled that one could cut it with a knife. For the remainder of the day, he and Molly carefully avoided one another. Conversation between them was very limited. Both of them spoke in clipped tones when they did address one another. Molly resembling a wounded doe when he'd told her he wasn't going anywhere instantly made Hudson feel like the Big Bad Wolf. But it wasn't all his fault. Molly had been out of line by suggesting that he pack up and call it a day. Clearly, she wasn't taking him seriously. She had no idea what this meant to him.

To be fair, he hadn't told anyone that he was back for good. He'd given up his place in Boston and put a few large items in a friend's garage until he could decide what to do with them. Hudson was all in regarding Humbled. He didn't know why it was so hard to be completely straightforward about the fact that Boston hadn't lived up to the hype. His college years had been a blast but he had soon outgrown the party scene. None of his romantic partners had ever been a good match. Working nonstop at his marketing firm had led to burnout. For so long he'd allowed his family to believe that he was content and living a perfect life.

A verse from Proverbs came to mind. *Pride goeth before destruction, and a haughty spirit before a fall.*

He would have to cast his pride aside and be completely honest with his family. Hudson prayed that in doing so a huge weight would be lifted off his shoulders. Pretending had never been his strong suit.

"You have a visitor," his coworker Estelle told him as she poked her head into the kitchen. Warm and inviting, Estelle was a woman in her early sixties who'd greeted him like an old friend earlier when Molly had introduced them. Her very presence had served as a nice buffer between him and Molly. Normally he shrugged off awkward situations, but his mind kept going back to the short period when they'd been dating. All this time, he'd managed to stuff down the memories of the way he had left Molly in the lurch. He wasn't proud of how he'd acted, but it had been an act of self-preservation. He had developed major feelings for her, which had scared him. Rather than risk putting himself in a difficult emotional situation, he'd done the immature thing and taken off for Boston.

"Me?" he asked Estelle. Maybe it was his grandfather stopping by to check on him. He knew that his parents were working at the tree farm all week, so it was doubtful they would swing by. Not to mention that his father would be the last one to do that. Even back at the house they still hadn't truly connected.

"Yes, you. Head out front, and I'll take over for you in here," she said, moving toward the blender.

He quickly left the kitchen and headed out front. Theo was standing by the counter looking around with wide eyes. A backpack was slung over his shoulder, and he was dressed in a thick winter parka and cords.

"Hud!" Theo called out, a grin stretching across his face. He threw himself against Hudson's chest and burrowed in.

"Hey, buddy. What are you doing here?" Hudson asked, tousling his hair.

Theo looked up at him, his eyes twinkling. "I wanted to come visit you after school let out," he said. "I didn't want to wait till dinnertime to see you."

He found himself getting a bit choked up. He'd missed out on so many years with his younger brother. Somehow he was going to try and make up for it. Clearly, Theo had missed his presence.

"Did you tell Mom you were coming?" He didn't want his family to worry about Theo's whereabouts.

"Yep," he answered. "Gramps is going to pick me up later. Maybe I can help you until then."

"I appreciate the offer, but it's my first day, and I've already got my feet to the fire." He wiggled his eyebrows. "I'm the new guy, so I've got a lot to learn."

Theo's eyes lit up. "Hey, Molly." He began to wave vigorously as she cleared tables nearby. Molly walked toward them, a huge smile etched on her face.

"Theo," she said, holding up her hand to him. Theo enthusiastically high-fived her. "You haven't been in here in a minute. Have you checked out the baked goods or did you want to look at the books?"

Theo's gaze darted to the baked goods in the display case. "I really came to say hi to Hud, but I'll never say no to baked goods."

Both he and Molly laughed at Theo's comment. His little brother had a serious sweet tooth. When he was younger, Hudson had always taken him for ice cream at his request during the coldest months of the year.

Molly winked at Theo. "Well, one of the perks of having a brother who works here is that you get complimentary treats."

"Does that mean free?" Theo asked, eyes widening.

"It sure does," Molly said, placing her finger on her lips. "Don't tell anyone. It's a little Humbled secret."

Theo made a twisting motion over his lips as if he was turning a key. "Your secret's safe with me."

Molly had such a sweet and gentle air with Theo. She was a natural with kids. A memory washed over him. *I'd like a house full of kids one day.* She'd told him that when they had been in high school. Hudson couldn't help but wonder if she still felt the same way. It wasn't hard to picture it since she had always been nurturing and kind.

"Why don't you tell Hud which ones you'd like, and he can package some up for you," Molly suggested. "Some for now and some for later."

Surprised by Molly's generosity, he led Theo behind the counter where he picked a lemon bar, two petits fours and a chocolate éclair. He selected a donut to eat in the shop.

"Why don't you take your break now so you can sit down with Theo," Molly suggested.

"Are you sure?" he asked, looking around. There had been a slight lull after lunchtime, but business was beginning to pick up again.

"Vinny just arrived, so he'll be manning the bookstore. Go ahead," she said, making a shooing motion with her hands.

Theo tugged on his arm. "Come on, Hud. There's a table by the window. We can watch the snow coming down."

Hudson led his brother to the table. A few minutes later Estelle came over and placed two hot cocoas down in front of them. "Molly said you might like some peppermint hot chocolate."

Theo bounced around in his seat and rubbed his hands together. "This is the best day ever."

"We aim to please," Estelle said, sharing a smile with Theo.

It was amazing how his baby brother had the entire town wrapped around his little finger.

As they sipped hot cocoa and split the donut between them, Theo filled Hudson in on all the goings-on at school and in Serenity Peak. He was just as much of a chatterbox as he'd been at that age. He let out a sigh as he watched a flurry of snowflakes fall from the sky. He'd really missed the Alaskan weather and the unpredictability of snow squalls. From his seat he had a view of the majestic Serenity Mountains. So many of his childhood adventures had taken place there—hiking, snow machining, sledding. He was looking forward to doing the same things with Theo.

After a short break, he headed back to work while Theo pulled out some homework to occupy himself with until their grandfather arrived.

"Thanks for being so kind to Theo," Hud said to Molly.

"It's no big deal." She shook her head. "I think being kind is second nature to most people. I'm a woman of faith, so it's important to me."

His own faith had been tested as of late, but he was still a believer. Losing Nana, along with his life in Boston falling apart, had made him question whether God was faithful. He prayed that being back home would strengthen his belief.

"It's just that things are pretty tense between us," he said, addressing the huge elephant in the room.

"And that has nothing to do with Theo. We're buddies. As far as I'm concerned, he's the most precious child in town." A hint of a smile played around her lips. "Maybe in all of Alaska."

He chuckled. "I can't dispute that statement. He's something else."

Just then Theo approached them, pointing at a spot above him. "Hey! You two are standing under the mistletoe. That means you have to kiss."

Hudson froze. Out of the mouths of babes. Could this day get any more awkward? Molly's cheeks flushed, and she opened then closed her mouth. Much like himself, she clearly didn't know how to shut down a twelve-year-old.

"Come on." Theo frowned. "Didn't Abel help the two of you make up from your fight?"

"Of course he did," Hud said.

"Well then, act like you like each other," Theo said, grinning. "Unless of course you don't."

"Why wouldn't we?" Molly murmured.

Hudson inwardly groaned. He didn't want to draw attention to any of the tension between him and Molly. As Molly had pointed out, she and Theo were buddies. The last thing he wanted was to place Theo in the middle of their dispute.

"See, we do like each other," Hud said as he turned toward Molly and leaned in, pressing a kiss against her cheek. The moment his lips touched her smooth skin, he knew that he'd made a big mistake. The smell of vanilla and cinnamon immediately rose to his nostrils. Molly's hair brushed across his face, and he fought the urge to bury his face in the silky locks. He quickly took a step back, confused as to what had come over him.

When he glanced at Molly, her expression was a mix of shock and awareness. She'd felt something too. He was certain of it.

Theo began clapping, his face lit up with a huge grin. "Now you're in the spirit of the holidays," he said.

Molly wrapped her arms around her middle and shifted

from one foot to the other before making her way back to the counter.

He forced himself to smile as if he hadn't just been sucker-punched. As if things weren't complicated enough between him and Molly, now there was this subtle shift in energy between them. It had been a long time since he'd felt this level of attraction, and of course, it had to be toward Molly, the very last woman in Alaska he wanted to feel something for.

Try as she might not to feel flustered, Molly couldn't calm down. Being so up close and personal with Hud had caused her stomach to do flip-flops. Her cheeks felt as if they were on fire. She didn't have a single doubt that they were red, thanks to her Irish roots. Molly always got flushed when she was embarrassed. She didn't have the skills to just carry on as if nothing had happened, so she swapped places with Estelle in the kitchen. Although she didn't say a word, Molly sensed that Estelle had picked up on her discomfort. She was a very intuitive and compassionate woman.

What had Hud been thinking? Granted, he'd just been playing along with Theo, but the gesture had left her feeling off-kilter and confused. It also served as a reminder that it had been ages since she'd been properly kissed. Sure, she'd had a few dates here and there, but there had been zero sparks. Not like there'd been with Hud. He had been the first man to tug on her heartstrings. It hadn't been love, but the feelings had been powerful. Who knows what might have happened if he'd stayed or kept in touch?

She vigorously shook her head in an attempt to rid herself of thoughts of him. Humbled had always been a haven for her, a place where she could be her authentic self and cast off all her troubles. In one day, all that had changed. She had been on pins and needles all morning, culminating in a kiss under the mistletoe.

It wasn't a real kiss, she reminded herself. As far as kisses went, it was fairly innocent.

But then why had her pulse quickened when his lips had touched her skin?

Why was the scent of his aftershave still lingering?

It wasn't as if she had been pining away for him all of these years. He'd barely been a thought, save for the fact that he'd missed Lillian's funeral. She, along with the entire town, had been shocked. Out of sight, out of mind, she thought. But now that he was back in Serenity Peak and working in such close proximity, it was impossible to put him in the back of her mind. And from what Hud had told her earlier, he wasn't going back to Beantown any time soon.

I'm here for the long haul.

Molly hadn't liked the sound of it. She'd heard the intensity in his voice as well as the undercurrent of anger. A part of her knew that Hud had been waving a red flag in her face with his bold statement. Just like when they were kids, he had always known what buttons to push.

Hud's words had hinted at the fact that once the thirty days of working together were over, he was still going to fight her for ownership of the shop. And that was a problem because she didn't trust him or his intentions. Lillian had died three years ago. Why had he waited so long to try and make a case for co-ownership? And how was Hud able to leave his job for a period of thirty days as if it wasn't a big deal?

"Molly." Hud's voice startled her out of her thoughts.

He had come into the kitchen without her even hearing him enter.

"My grandad came to pick up Theo. He wanted me to tell you goodbye," Hud said, leaning against the counter. "I just figured we should talk."

Oh no. Was he going to mention the mistletoe cheek kiss? Why did this day seem like it was never-ending? Her embarrassment was at an all-time high.

She held up her hands. "No worries. We don't need to talk about the kiss."

Hud's eyes went wide. "The kiss? Umm, no I didn't want to talk about that. Unless you do, of course. I mean—" He fumbled with his words.

"No," she said in a raised voice. "It's not necessary."

Talking about the kiss was the very last thing Molly wanted to do.

"Actually, I would love to sit down with you and talk over some ideas about the shop," he said.

Molly felt her pulse race. Ideas? Humbled was her baby. Who did Hud think he was butting in like this and trying to put his stamp on her establishment? This was how he planned to take over, by sliding in with his ideas.

Just breathe. Hear him out.

"I—I'm not used to brainstorming with anyone about Humbled," she blurted out. She might as well be honest with him.

"That's understandable," he said. "But I do have eight years of experience in marketing, and I'm coming in with a fresh pair of eyes."

Hmm. He did have practical experience that he was bringing to the table. She couldn't turn a blind eye to that fact. Part of being a business owner was keeping one's eye on ways to improve the bottom line.

"Anything we discuss will be in order to maximize Humbled's potential and to ensure that sales are rolling in."

Molly bit her lip. "Sales are good, but I would love to see growth," she admitted. That had been the challenge with the shop. Serenity Peak was a fairly small town. Thanks to Sugar Works, tourism had flourished. Although the shop benefited from tourists like the Dennisons, Molly knew there were many other avenues to pursue to increase revenue. She had been trying to figure out how to draw customers from neighboring towns to her establishment with limited success.

The idea of giving any measure of control over to Hud caused an ache in her chest. She didn't know why this was so hard for her. It would simply be tossing ideas around to see if anything stuck. The likelihood was that none of Hud's ideas would hit the mark. After all, he didn't know Humbled like she did. While she'd been devoting her life to revitalizing and running the shop, he'd been living his best life thousands of miles away.

"I can help with that," Hud said. "Trust me, I know I'm not getting any awards as employee of the month. I've got a lot to learn. But there are things I can contribute to Humbled."

"With your marketing expertise," Molly said.

Hud nodded. "I can't see any harm in brainstorming ideas. No risk, no reward."

He was right. Anything that benefited Humbled was in her best interest. She could always let him down easy if need be.

"Okay. Can you stay for a bit after work one day this week? Maybe we can have a brainstorming session then," she suggested. "And I can ask Estelle and Vinny to join us. They know this place inside and out." If Hud stuck around, he would discover that they were the most loyal and hardworking employees in the world.

"Sounds good," he said. "Thanks for being open to what I had to say. I know this situation hasn't been easy."

They locked eyes, and for an instant she caught a glimpse of the old Hud, the one who'd shown his vulnerabilities and opened up to her. During their brief romance Hud had opened up to her about his hopes and dreams, as well as his fears that he would never gain his father's approval. Molly didn't want to let her guard down with him. Having done so once before, she knew that Hud was a risk.

"It hasn't been," she acknowledged. "But we agreed to thirty days, so I'm committed to that. Keeping my word means something to me." She wondered if he was committed as well. Although he seemed intense about the shop, she knew from firsthand experience that Hud put his own interests first. If he got bored with being a shopkeeper, he might just pack up and head back to Massachusetts.

She was praying for discernment about trusting Hud.

Molly had no intention of allowing him to pull the rug out from under her. If he did, she would have no one to blame but herself.

Chapter Seven

Hud was a different type of tired after a few days of working at Humbled. His entire body ached from stocking shelves, carrying boxes of books and lifting chairs and kitchen items. He had a newfound respect for this line of work. After getting out of bed, he took a hot shower and got dressed for work. He hadn't been wearing a suit after the first day, having realized that doing so made him stick out like a sore thumb, when in reality all he wanted to do was fit in.

Sitting down for breakfast around the large dining-room table was hectic and heartwarming. He hadn't known just how much he'd missed his family until this very moment. Loud voices. Squabbles. The smell of his mother's downhome cooking. The blue plates they always used for breakfast—the color of forget-me-nots, Alaska's state flower.

He couldn't remember the last time he'd prayed over a meal back in Boston. How had he allowed himself to stray so far away from his faith?

Lord, please forgive me for my shortcomings. I've strayed away from Your path. I promise to do better, with Your grace.

Once he finished his meal, Hud took his plate and utensils, headed into the kitchen and placed them in the dishwasher. He put on his winter parka and poked his head into the dining room.

"See you later, alligators," he called out to his family. A chorus of voices yelled goodbye, creating a full feeling in his heart. He lingered for a moment in the doorway just watching them. Everyone was sitting there with the exception of his father, who always got an early start every morning with the tree farm. It was just as well, Hud thought. They were like oil and water. His dad hadn't shown a single sign that he was happy about his return. Clearly, they were still at an impasse. Hudson wasn't even sure why his father was angry at him. It just seemed as if he'd always disapproved of every move Hudson made.

His grandfather gripped his arm just as he was about to leave the house. "Hudson, can we talk for a moment?"

"I'd love to, but I'm heading out to work," he said. "If I'm late, Molly might think I'm not serious about this arrangement." He hated to turn his grandfather down, but he needed to keep his eyes on the prize. They could catch up later.

"That's exactly what's on my mind, grandson. This business with Humbled. How about I drive you into town, and then I can pick you up at the end of the day?" He chuckled. "Theo will love coming to get you and taking a ride in my truck."

Bert's antique truck was legendary here in Serenity Peak. A 1952 light blue Chevy, the vehicle was his grandfather's pride and joy. He didn't drive it often, but when he did it was a big deal.

"Now how can I turn down an offer like that?" Hudson asked.

Bert grinned. "Let me just grab my keys and coat."

Minutes later they were in the truck and driving away

from the family compound. His grandad had always been a masterful driver. He'd learned to drive at thirteen on these same Alaskan roads. Being in the passenger seat was nice. The scenery was beautiful, with snow as far as the eye could see.

"So, what's up? You wanted to talk to me?" Hudson asked, turning his gaze toward Bert.

Gramps let out a snort. "What's up? You come waltzing back into town after a four-year absence dropping bombshells and then ask me that question."

"I know it's a bit shocking," he said, sighing. The last thing he'd ever wanted to do was upset Gramps. Maybe that was part of the reason he'd kept his plans under wraps. Although they had discussed the unfairness of the situation when Hud had managed her affairs, Bert hadn't known the direction of his thoughts. This plan had been several years in the making. Maybe it was selfish, but he hadn't wanted his grandfather to tell him no.

Bert chuckled. "I know you, Hudson, which means I'm not in the least bit shocked. But, at the very least, you could have given me a heads-up. A phone call. An email. Anything."

He ducked his head. "I'm sorry you felt blindsided. I was so wrapped up trying to rectify this situation that I had blinders on. And I couldn't help but think that you would choose the path of least resistance." He sucked in a breath. "All I want to do is make sure that Nana's legacy is in place. How can that be wrong?"

His grandad's grip on the wheel tightened. "It's not wrong at all. Lillian deserves to be recognized for her contributions to Humbled. It's long overdue. I have regrets about dropping the matter all those years ago."

A sense of relief flowed through him. He cared deeply about his grandfather's opinion of him.

"So you approve of what I'm doing?" Hudson asked, studying his grandad's face in profile. "You're not upset?"

"Not at all, but I do have some questions. Why now? After all this time?"

It was a reasonable question with a complicated answer.

"You sent me Nana's personal journals after she passed away, and I finally went through all of them."

"I sent you those journal entries because they were too painful for me to go through after we lost her. Something told me they might be important."

"I had no idea she had spent so much time working on the shop. She was basically involved from the ground up. Concept. Layout. Construction. Hiring." He ran a hand over his face. "There's even an item on the menu named after her."

Bert nodded. "The Lillian. Scrambled eggs with sausage on a croissant. My personal favorite."

According to customers, it was savory and delicious. One of the favorite items on the menu. Still and all, a sandwich was nothing in the scheme of things. His grandmother deserved more!

"I must admit that I did a double take when I saw it," Hudson said. "It's just another piece of evidence for the case. Nana is imbedded in every nook and cranny of Humbled, yet she never got her due."

A few moments of silence stretched out between them. He had the feeling that Bert was thinking about his bride. They had been a true love story, and he knew how deeply Gramps missed her. Nearly sixty years of marriage without a single night apart. It would be like walking around without a part of one's soul.

"And you still intend to take this to court even though you're working with Molly now?" Gramps asked. Surprise radiated from his voice.

"Thirty days can't fix what's broken," Hudson said, making a face. "It's way deeper than that."

"I agree, but Molly shouldn't have to bear the brunt of decisions that were made before she was even born."

Hudson frowned. "Whose side are you on?" he asked.

"You already know the answer to that," Gramps said, "but I want you to proceed without any blinders on. Some things you can't take back."

As they arrived in the downtown area, signs of the holiday season were everywhere. Strands of evergreen were looped around the columns of the town library. Every lamppost in town had been decorated to make them resemble red and white striped candy canes. A big evergreen tree sat bare in the town square, awaiting the annual tree lighting ceremony.

"That's one of ours," Gramps said, glancing over at the tree. "A Fraser fir."

Hudson let out a low whistle. "It sure is a beauty."

Judging by the way he was beaming, his grandad was pretty pleased with the tree.

"By the way, Hud, I know that you're hiding something about Boston. I can still read you like a book," Bert said. "Not sure what's going on, but I don't think your life there is all that fantastic."

He nearly let out a gasp. Gramps was a bloodhound by nature. He could sniff out a secret from a mile away.

Hudson sighed. "It's complicated," he admitted.

Moments later they pulled up right next to the shop. There were no lights glinting from inside, which meant that he was the first one to arrive this morning. Molly had given him a set of keys so he wouldn't be left outside in the cold to wait for her.

"I'll be here at five," Gramps told him.

"Thanks for the ride and the conversation. I've missed these moments."

Bert clapped him on the shoulder. "You've been greatly missed as well."

"I'm going to leave before things get too mushy," Hudson said.

The sound of Bert's laughter rang in his ears as he exited the truck. As he walked away, Gramps beeped the horn, the same way he'd done when Hudson was a kid.

He took the keys out of his pocket and stepped toward the door. Just then Molly walked up looking stylish in a red parka and matching hat. She had a newspaper in her hand.

"Morning," he said, admiring her understated beauty. She never wore makeup other than a slight sheen on her lips, yet she was stunning.

"Good morning." She held up the town newspaper, The Serenity Tribune. "Just checking in on local news. I see you're traveling in style," she said, her gaze trailing after the truck.

"Gramps sure loves that old Chevy," he noted.

"I hope he's not upset with me about my showing up at your home the other day," Molly said, frowning. "I was operating on pure adrenaline."

Hudson scoffed. "Are you serious? That's probably the most exciting thing that's happened to Gramps in years."

Molly chuckled. "I hope not. If that's the case, he needs to get out more."

"Shall I do the honors?" he asked, holding up the keys. Molly nodded and he opened up the shop, waving Molly in before he stepped inside. The aroma of cinnamon and bread filled the air. It was almost as if the scents were imbedded in the walls. As far as he was concerned, it was the best smell on earth.

"I'm working in the bookstore today, right?" he asked. He'd been looking forward to spending more time on that side of Humbled. He was finding that working in the bookstore was a lot more laid back than the café.

"Yes, you're in there all day for the most part," Molly told him. "With backup from Vinny so you can grab lunch and breaks."

"Awesome," he said. He wasn't going to admit to Molly that he preferred the slower pace on that side. It wasn't that he was work shy, but it was going to take a while to master the intricacies of the café. Yesterday he'd been thrown for a loop when someone had ordered a tongue twister of a drink. A peppermint frappé, decaf, with oat milk and whipped cream. Somehow he'd managed to fill the order, but it had been extremely challenging. What ever happened to ordering a simple black coffee? These days it was all about the frills and the extras.

Estelle entered the shop, all bundled up in a long winter coat, wool hat and sturdy winter boots. With snow in the forecast, they were all bracing to see how much was coming. "Brr. It's cold out there," she said, shivering.

"Let me take those off your hands," Hudson said, plucking the baking tins from her grip and moving them toward the display case.

"Thanks, Hudson. It's nice to have an extra pair of hands around here," Estelle said as she began taking off her outerwear.

He wasn't sure if Molly agreed that his presence at Humbled was an asset, but maybe he was growing on her. They had both seemed to recognize that they needed to put aside their animosity for at least thirty days and focus on the business.

"I'm going to go stock the shelves with the books that arrived yesterday." Hudson began to walk toward the bookstore. "I think that new thriller, *Denali*, is going to be a big seller."

"I love thrillers, but they keep me up at night," Estelle said, shuddering.

"Oh, Hud," Molly called out. "I forgot to tell you that we're expecting a group of kindergarten students today in the bookstore."

He turned around to face her. "Kindergarteners?" he asked, hoping he'd misheard her. He loved little ones as much as the next person, but his morning was going to be spent running after a group of crumb snatchers.

"Yep." Molly winked at him. "I sure hope you ate your Wheaties this morning."

Molly couldn't stop smiling as she heard the loud chatter of little voices emanating from the bookstore. Hudson sure had his hands full with the visiting kindergartners, who were full of energy and laughter. She imagined it was a little bit of controlled chaos over there.

This was a good lesson for Hud, Molly thought. She was probably being petty, but in their youth he'd always had a tendency to act like a know-it-all. The truth was he didn't have any practical experience with running a shop and she sensed that he was aware of his inexperience. She had to admit that he was constantly surprising her, though. Yesterday at their team meeting, his suggestions had been fresh and innovative. Both Estelle and Vinny had been over the moon about his ideas. Honestly, she had felt a twinge of envy. He'd just waltzed back into town and was already knocking it out of the park.

His concepts were fun. He'd even suggested a series of singles events involving baking and books. Weekly knitting meet ups. Establishing a strong social media presence online. Such amazing ideas! Meanwhile, her concepts seemed basic, especially when compared to Hud's creativity. Flyers and word of mouth couldn't compete with more innovative campaigns. Molly had opened up a social media account years ago, but it had gotten stale. Admittedly, she hadn't put in the required time and effort to make it shine.

It's about Humbled, she reminded herself. Not your bruised ego.

Filled with curiosity about what was going on next door, Molly entered the bookstore and stood out of view as Hudson acted out *How the Grinch Stole Christmas*. The children were animated, laughing and grinning as Hud made faces, spoke in a booming Grinch voice and brilliantly acted out his part. He had the entire group mesmerized.

As he finished and took a bow, the kids began clapping and loudly pleading for more. She shook her head, feeling astounded. He seemed to be in his element with the kids, even though he'd clearly been dreading the experience earlier. She had to hand it to him. Hud really was successful in so many areas. A true Renaissance man.

She walked back to the café, greeting customers along the way. There was such a wonderful holiday vibe pulsing in the air. Her favorite part of owning a café was the aromas of baked goods and the sense of community everyone experienced within these walls. There were a few additional touches she wanted to make in order for the place to pop with Christmas cheer. There were festive bakery items she couldn't wait to showcase—red velvet cheesecake squares, chocolate yule log cake, white chocolate gingerbread cookies and snowman cupcakes. She wanted to string up some pine garlands and vintage ornaments to enhance the Yuletide atmosphere.

"Hello, Molly," a customer called out to her.

She turned her head in the direction of the voice, smiling at the graceful woman standing a few feet away. With mahogany-colored skin and shoulder length black hair, Jada Locke was a lovely woman who radiated kindness. Her twin sons, Caden and Brody, had grown up with Molly. The entire family was beloved. She vaguely recalled Hud being close friends with Brody.

"Hi, Jada," Molly said, leaning in for a hug. Her sweet friend smelled distinctly of a fresh bouquet of flowers.

Jada was one of her top customers. A few times a week, she came into Humbled to drink coffee, browse through the bookshelves and sit at a table working on her knitting.

"What are you working on today?" Molly asked, quickly noticing her needles and yarn sticking out of her colorful tote bag.

"Well, I'm working on some baby booties. Hopefully my boys will take the hint," she said, winking. "I'm dying for them to meet their other halves and settle down."

Hmm. Maybe Hud was on to something about hosting events for singles at Humbled.

"Let me ask you something, Jada. We're trying to host more events at Humbled, and we're thinking about a weekly meet up for knitters. Is that something you'd be interested in?"

"Absolutely," Jada said, sounding enthused. "And I have several friends who would join in as well. It would be great to have a place to connect with a knitting circle."

Molly clapped her hands together. "Thanks for the feedback. We're also thinking about hosting a holiday mixer for singles. Lots of mistletoe and peppermint hot cocoa."

"I love that you're mixing things up," Jada said. "Kudos for being so innovative."

As Molly walked away, all she could think about was the fact that Hud was the one responsible for these ideas and not her. She had plenty of her own concepts, but she was too chicken to put them out there. She should have laid them all out on the table at the meeting yesterday. Instead, she'd sat and listened to Hud's wonderful concepts, while sitting on her own.

What was she so afraid of? Maybe all this time she had been playing it safe, so afraid of disappointing her family that she wasn't taking any risks. *No risk, no reward.* Hadn't Hud said that the other day?

A short while later, the group of school children, led by Hud and their teacher, paraded out of the bookstore, each one carrying a goody bag of books and candy canes. From what Molly could see, they'd immensely enjoyed themselves. And judging by the ear-to-ear grin on Hud's face, he'd had a blast as well. He stood in the doorway, waving to the kids as they stepped out into the snowy afternoon.

"Pretty sweet, huh?" Estelle asked as she peered over Molly's shoulder.

"Enough to give you a toothache," Molly said dryly.

Estelle playfully jabbed her in the side. "Come on, Molly. I know Hud put you in an impossible situation with Humbled, but even in the short time he's been with us, he's been pretty great."

"You're right, Estelle. He's been better than expected. However, I need to be pragmatic. Once this month is over, I might find myself in a courtroom." Just the thought of it made her stomach clench. In the weeks ahead she might need to start preparing for a court battle, starting with hiring an attorney and gathering information to support her case.

Estelle patted her on the back. "I know it must be worrisome, but perhaps there's a way to resolve things outside of the courtroom. Hud seems to really be invested in Humbled's success. He's not simply trying to be a thorn in your side."

Estelle made a good point. Hud was less antagonistic than when he'd first arrived in town. And he did seem to genuinely care about the shop.

"That's true. He had some amazing ideas for engaging more customers. And I think we should implement some of his plans right away. In particular, I'm feeling enthused about his idea of having special events for singles." Seeing Jada's enthusiasm had lit a fire inside her. Renovating the place had simply been a first step. Hosting events would be another step toward increasing their customer base. And if folks fell in love in the process at their singles events, it would be a wonderful thing.

"That's great," Estelle said. "A singles event would generate a lot of buzz."

"That's what we want," Molly said. "Business is good, but it could always be better."

Estelle gave her a thumbs up before walking away.

Just then Hud came over. "Hey! You won't believe what I found," he said, holding up a book. The blue coloring on the cover was distinctive, along with the characters.

"The Hardy Boys," Molly said. "That series is very popular, along with vintage Nancy Drews. Collectibles even. They're some of our best sellers."

"Guess what? I'm going to buy this one," Hud said. "I loved these books when I was growing up. They were the best. My dyslexia made reading difficult, but once I progressed it became a favorite pastime."

She had remembered about his dyslexia after the chili incident but hadn't wanted to bring the issue up. In his younger years, it had led to a great deal of frustration.

Hud began to flip through the pages. "I remember this story!" His features were animated as he took a trip down memory lane. He actually resembled a big kid. Molly felt a sense of nostalgia sweep over her. Despite their current day tensions, Hud had been a part of her childhood. Skinned knees and sled dog rides. Birthday parties and graduations. They shared a connection.

"No need to buy it. Just consider it a welcome home gift," Molly said.

"Seriously? Thank you, Molly." He tucked the book under his arm.

"You're quite welcome. It's the least I could do since you've been working so hard."

He moved toward her so that only a few inches stood between them. "Tell the truth. I'm growing on you, aren't I, Molly?"

The way he said it made her chuckle. "Growing on me like a rash," she said.

Hud let out a deep-throated laugh. "I guess I asked for that one."

"You sure did," she said, smiling. "By the way, let's not wait on getting these events started. I'd like to put together some flyers and get the word out."

"I can handle the flyers," he offered. "I know a few tricks of the trade to make 'em pop. And I can get some social media engagement started."

"I'll write down the particulars about dates and times. We can start this week with the knitting circle and then move on to the singles mixer." She looked over at Jada, who was happily knitting and enjoying a drink at her table. "I can ask Mrs. Locke to help us spread the word to her knitting friends."

Hud turned his head to follow her gaze. A smile was tugging at his lips. "I used to be a fixture at the Lockes' house growing up. I'd love to see Caden and Brody again."

"You should definitely reach out to them before they hear you're back through the grapevine." Clearly, Hud hadn't kept in touch with the brothers over the years.

"Excuse me, Molly, I'm going to go over and say hello," he said.

Molly watched Hud as he beat a fast path toward Jada's table. Mrs. Locke stood up from her seat and wrapped Hud up in a warm embrace. It was a heartwarming moment that made her think about how the townsfolk in Serenity Peak were bound together by invisible ties. Even if they were frayed, they still endured. She hoped Hud would realize that no matter how far he'd traveled away from home, he was still part of the community.

And maybe he would realize that his lawsuit against her totally went against the values of Serenity Peak. The holiday season was a time for goodwill and harmony. Love and light.

Surely Hud wouldn't do anything to disrupt that.

Chapter Eight

"I can't believe you're back, Hud."

Brody Locke, his childhood best friend, was sitting across from him at Northern Lights, a popular local restaurant. Situated on a cliff overlooking Kachemak Bay, the establishment was a favorite destination among townsfolk and tourists. It didn't hurt that there was also an amazing view of the Serenity mountains. The eatery served some of the best local seafood in the area. The place was oozing with Christmas charm. A huge pine wreath hung on the wall. Twinkling lights were strewn around miniature decorative trees. The aroma of cinnamon hung in the air.

Hudson had called his friend the day before, hoping to reconnect after seeing his mother at Humbled. Brody had immediately invited him to dinner so they could catch up. He hadn't hesitated to say yes.

Hudson hadn't thought about all the attention he would draw with his appearance at the popular restaurant. Heads had literally turned the moment he entered the place, with numerous people approaching him, as well as waving from their tables.

"It's been a long time, hasn't it?" Hudson asked. He felt incredibly guilty about not keeping in touch. He hoped Brody didn't feel as if he'd turned his back on him.

"Too long," Brody said. "I saw you about three and a half years ago when you visited, but we didn't get to hang out or talk."

"I've been really bad about staying connected," he admitted. "Some kind of friend I've been." Although it was a hard admission, he was trying to be transparent. Being back in Serenity Peak was forcing him to take a long look at his past actions. Even though it wasn't pretty at times, he knew that doing so was important.

"I understand," Brody said. "You were so set on getting away from Serenity Peak and creating a new life for yourself." He locked eyes with him. "Honestly, I wasn't sure you'd ever come back."

Brody was alluding to the clashes with his father. That had been Hudson's true impetus for going to school in Boston, far away from his dad's disapproval and overbearing ways. He had been such close friends with Brody that he'd confided in him about the difficult father-son relationship. Brody had always been a great listening ear.

Their waiter, Fred, brought their entrees over—a bison burger with sweet potato fries for Brody and grilled salmon for Hudson with a cup of corn chowder. They dug in to their meals, while still making time for conversation.

"Well, I've never been able to shake off this town," Hudson said. "It's in my bloodstream, if you know what I mean." No matter how he'd tried over the years to tamp down the feelings, he'd always ached to get back to Serenity Peak.

Brody grinned. "Of course I do. Every time I go out on Fishful Thinking as a member of Judah's crew, I think how blessed I am to live in Alaska."

A commercial fisherman, Brody worked in a profession

that had endured in Serenity Peak for generations. Salmon, halibut and crab were staples of the industry in Alaska.

"Do you still love being a fisherman?" he asked him. There was something so admirable about dedicating one's professional life to one of the oldest industries in Alaska.

"I do," Brody said. "I know that probably doesn't make sense to you since you went the college route, but it gives me a sense of purpose."

"It totally makes sense to me, especially since you're doing what you love." What Hudson wouldn't give to know that he was living out his purpose. He'd never experienced that in Boston. His marketing job had made him miserable.

"So, how's life in Boston? Are you doing what you love?" Brody asked. He was leaning across the table, eagerly awaiting his answer.

For so long he'd been pretending that his life was fabulous, when in reality the fast-paced Boston lifestyle had left him deflated and unhappy. Even during his short time at Humbled, he'd been feeling reinvigorated and inspired.

"I haven't been happy in a long time," he admitted. "You're the first person I'm telling this to, but I've come back for good."

Brody's face lit up. "That's amazing, bro. I heard you were working at Humbled, which surprised me a bit. It all makes sense now."

"Yeah, I am. It's been interesting. My grandmother had a big role in creating the shop so it makes me feel more connected with her." He didn't fill Brody in on his having served Molly with legal papers or the dispute about ownership. He and Molly had agreed to keep that news private. He trusted Brody, but he didn't want to break his promise to Molly.

Brody narrowed his gaze. "Is that why you've stayed away so long? Your grandmother?"

He chewed and swallowed a bite of his fish before responding. "I felt so guilty that I wasn't here when she passed. It really messed me up." He let out a sigh. "I hope that by coming back I can make things right." That was what his return was all about. Redemption. Creating a legacy.

"Hud, you're a part of this town. Now and for always. That won't ever change," Brody told him. "I know a whole bunch of the fellas will want to see you and reconnect. Caden most of all. He's talked of little else since he flew you in to town."

Caden was Brody's twin. Fraternal twins who shared big personalities and a superficial resemblance. Both had varying shades of brown skin and athletic frames. Caden was a bit taller, Brody more muscular. They had all been as thick as thieves growing up, running around and creating havoc here in town. He hadn't realized until this very moment how much he'd missed those friendships. Hudson had a gaping hole in his heart that could only be filled with the people and places in this beloved place.

"Lots of our friend group have settled down. Ryan married Skye and they're raising a daughter. Luke and Destiny are hitched and running a K-9 business. Guess we're all growing up," Brody said.

"I can't even imagine." Hudson let out a laugh. He felt so far away from making a lifetime commitment to a woman. Had he ever been in love? He still wasn't sure. The closest he'd come had been with Molly, but he had taken off to Boston when things became too intense. Hudson had been running away from romantic entanglements ever since. His girlfriend, Lara, had accused him of being emotionally unavailable, which upon closer scrutiny, had most likely been true.

"So, how's it been working with Molly?" Brody was one of the few people who'd known about his and Molly's brief relationship.

Hudson looked away from his friend's probing gaze. When it came to Molly, he tended to be all over the place. His feelings were a mix of so many emotions. He still felt angry toward the Truitt family for cutting his grandmother out of the business. But working alongside Molly was allowing him to get reacquainted with her. She had such a strong work ethic and a warm disposition. Even though he hadn't shown her any grace when he'd first arrived back in town, she'd bent over backward to be kind.

Was he getting soft? Or was his past with Molly influencing him? She'd once been very special to him. He couldn't ignore the fact that she still mattered. After all, they had known each other all their lives.

"Molly is great," he said. "Better than I deserve," he muttered. All of a sudden he was feeling badly about things. Was he making the right move in fighting for a slice of the shop? Or was he simply stirring up a hornet's nest to assuage his own conscience?

Brody wiggled his eyebrows. "You two have a lot of history. Who knows what might happen?"

Hudson chuckled. "Sounds like you've been spending too much time with Ryan and Luke. Not everyone couples up. Molly and I are just friends," he said. More like frenemies, he thought. Not that Brody needed to know that. Best that everyone view them as old friends who were working together. Explaining their situation further would be TMI.

Brody wiped his mouth with a napkin before placing it on his empty plate. "Oh, that's what they all say," he said, making a face. "Unexpected things happen during the holidays."

Hudson shook his head. He wasn't even going to entertain Brody's fanciful notions. Anything happening between him and Molly was out of the question. Although they were working together and making nice, they were still at odds over the fate of Humbled. He didn't imagine that they would work out their issues in a period of thirty days.

Despite twinges of guilt, he really wasn't the sort of person to give up the battle before it even started. Hud knew one thing for certain—he was the only person who could right certain wrongs.

And he wasn't about to stop fighting for his grandmother's legacy. Not by a long shot.

Molly smiled as she looked at the mockup of the flyers Hud had created. They were vibrant and festive—red, green and white in honor of the holiday season. Two brand-new events—knitters and singles looking to make connections. A feeling of excitement rose up inside of her. Even if just a few people showed up to each, it would be well worth it. The more she'd thought about it, the more Molly had begun to realize that Hud was right. This was the way businesses grew. Word of mouth simply wasn't enough these days.

She would have to give Hud the green light about the flyers. It would be smart to get them circulated as fast as possible, as well as posting on social media about the events. Molly was getting excited. She had a few recipes that she wanted to roll out for these special events. One was a very special spice cake she'd created in her grandmother's memory.

All of a sudden she heard the buzz of her cell phone. It had been pinging nonstop for the last half hour. She walked over to the kitchen counter and picked up her phone where it was charging. A quick glance revealed that the incoming call was from Doc Poppy.

"Hey, Poppy," she said. "How's it going?" Poppy was a local doctor who also happened to be a pal of hers. Warm and generous, Poppy was known for her compassionate care.

"Hi, Molly. I hope you're doing all right. I'm calling about Phineas."

She inwardly groaned. Her grandfather had a habit of giving his doctor a hard time. Whether it was taking his medicine or getting his required vaccines, he always put up a fuss.

"What's he done this time?" Molly asked, feeling exasperated.

"Well, he had an appointment with me this morning that he didn't show up for. I've called him a few times, but he isn't answering," Poppy said.

"Oh no," Molly said. "That's not like him." He might be a difficult patient, but he always showed up for his scheduled appointments.

"I don't mean to alarm you, but maybe someone can run by to check on him," Poppy suggested. "I would do it myself, but I've got back-to-back patients."

Molly bit her lip. This was definitely concerning news. She had a sinking feeling in her gut that wouldn't ease up.

"I understand. Thanks, Poppy, for letting me know," Molly said before ending the call. She immediately dialed her grandfather's cell phone, and when he didn't answer, called the landline. With no answer on either line, Molly began to feel frantic. Had something happened to him? He was all alone at the house without anyone checking in on him during the day. Anything could have happened and no one would know.

Just then Hud stepped into the kitchen with a tray full of dirty dishes.

Molly was pacing up and down the length of the room, eaten up by worry.

"Molly, is something wrong?" Hud asked as he deposited the tray next to the sink.

She couldn't even pretend as if things were fine. Her stomach was in knots, and a dozen different scenarios were playing around in her head. What if he'd fallen and hit his head or passed out?

"My grandfather had a doctor's appointment that he missed this morning. Hud, that's not like him at all. I can't reach him by phone." She could hear her voice trembling. "I'm getting worried."

"Can you ask a neighbor to pop in to check on him?" he asked, brow furrowed.

She shook her head. "Normally my parents are right there to check in on him, but they extended their trip to visit with friends. I'm just not sure who to call." Tears pooled in her eyes. Molly hadn't yet told her parents about the potential lawsuit since she'd wanted them to enjoy their time away without any worries. Now it felt as if things were piling up.

Molly was normally stoic. She didn't like to wear her emotions on her sleeve. It was hard to be vulnerable in front of Hud, but concern over her grandfather's well-being was her main focus.

"Why don't we drive over there? Let me take you, Molls," he suggested, using her childhood nickname. "Please let me help."

Surprise flowed through her at his offer. "Really? You would do that?"

He placed his hand on her shoulder. "Of course I would. You're in no shape to drive, and the midday rush is over. I'm sure Vinny and Estelle will be fine."

"I won't argue with you on that point." She held out her shaking hands. "I can't imagine driving. I'm a bundle of nerves."

Hud moved toward the coat rack and grabbed his parka, along with her bright pink one.

"Why don't we take my truck? It's suited for snow and ice," Molly said. The streets leading to Pops's house were winding back roads. Black ice was known to be the cause of many accidents in town.

Hud held out her jacket for her, and she slid her arms through the sleeves. She turned around to face him, feeling such a strong burst of gratitude that she almost hugged him.

"I appreciate this. After losing Gran I don't take anything for granted."

"Nor should you." Hudson nodded. "I understand. Tomorrow isn't promised."

Tomorrow isn't promised. Gran used to say that very same thing all the time. At this moment it deeply resonated with her. Losing Eva had been heart-wrenching. If anything happened to Phineas, it would serve as a gut punch to her loved ones.

Molly needed to get to her grandfather's house as soon as possible.

Please, Lord, watch over Pops and shelter him in Your loving arms.

Chapter Nine

Once they got outside, Molly led him to her truck. Hud knew he should purchase his own vehicle and ditch the rental. He needed an all-terrain truck with tire chains for these difficult Alaskan roads. He got behind the wheel and revved the engine as Molly provided the directions. Although he knew Molly was operating with a deep sense of urgency, Hudson needed to drive carefully on these slick back roads. Things could get dicey in an instant if he drove too fast. The ride was scenic, even though the falling snow lessened visibility. Thankfully, Bert had taught him to be a skilled driver in his teenaged years. It had served as a bonding experience that made them even closer.

"Make the right at the Moose Crossing sign, and it's down the road on the left," Molly instructed.

"It's all coming back to me," Hudson said, remembering all the times Nana had brought him to the Truitts' home. As a kid he'd played with Molly while their two grandmothers socialized and had tea parties. He wondered if Molly recalled those days when they'd played hide-and-seek and jacks.

"Here it is," Molly called out as a log cabin home came into view. Not a single light emanated from the house in the darkness. "Pull up right in front," Molly instructed as she practically jumped from the truck. He quickly turned off the vehicle and joined her at the front door. His own adrenaline was racing like wildfire through his veins.

Without even stopping to knock, Molly took the keys from her bag and opened up the door. Hud followed right behind her as she called out to Phineas.

"Pops! It's Molly. Where are you?"

He couldn't help but notice that there were no holiday adornments. No Christmas tree was anywhere in sight. Hudson remembered a home brimming with holiday cheer—poinsettias by the fireplace, a fully trimmed Christmas tree and the scent of pine drifting throughout the place.

"Molly," a muffled voice responded.

"Pops!" She glanced over at Hudson. "I can't tell where his voice is coming from. Can you?"

He listened intently as Phineas called out to Molly again. "I'm down here, Molly."

"Over there," Hudson said, pointing toward a door at the back of the kitchen.

They both raced over toward it, with Molly wrenching it open. In the dim light, he could see Molly's grandfather at the bottom of the steps sitting on a chair.

"Whatever you do, don't close that door behind you," he said. "That's how I got into this mess."

"I'll hold the door," Hudson said. "You can check to see if he's injured."

"Thanks," Molly said as she descended the stairs. He could see her bent over at the waist checking on her grandfather. "Pops, are you hurt?"

"The only thing hurt is my pride for being so foolish as to get myself locked down here," Phineas grumbled. At least he sounded like he was in one piece, Hudson thought.

He knew Molly had feared the worst, which was understandable. She'd already suffered one huge loss.

"Let's head back upstairs," Molly said. She held Phineas's hand and pulled him to a standing position. All in all, he seemed to be in good shape as he mounted the stairs.

Hud stood at the top of the stairs still holding the door open as they emerged from the basement.

Phineas did a double take when he saw him up close. "Hudson Doherty! Is that you?"

Hudson heard a slight edge to Mr. Truitt's voice. "Yes, sir, it's me," he said.

Phineas made a face. "I don't like the things I've been hearing about you from my girl here."

Hudson gulped. The older man had never been shy. He put it all out there, leaving Hud feeling a bit speechless and a bit guilty.

"Pops, why don't we go to the kitchen and get you some water or tea," Molly suggested, looping her arm through his. Hud shut the basement door and followed closely behind, watching the sweet dynamic between them. Phineas sat down at the table as Molly put the kettle on.

"Take a load off," Phineas instructed, patting the table. "I don't bite."

Hud wasn't so sure about that. Phineas had always been known as temperamental.

He sat down just as Molly placed saucers in front of them along with a tin of peppermint tea, sugar and milk.

Molly placed a hand on Phineas's shoulder. "What were you doing downstairs? Anything could have happened if you'd slipped."

"I'm not an invalid," Phineas protested. "I'm old, not feeble."

"No one said you were," Molly said, letting out a sigh.

She poured hot water into their cups so they could each prepare their tea. Hudson took a long swig of his to fortify himself. Something told him that he would soon be on the hot seat.

Phineas turned his attention to Hudson, fiercely glowering at him. "It takes a lot of nerve to show up here after what you pulled."

He reminded himself to stay calm. As an elder, Phineas was a man to respect. They could agree to disagree.

Hud took another sip of his tea. "All I did was stick up for my Nana and what's owed her memory. If that's wrong, I'm not sure that I want to be right."

Her grandfather let out a snort.

"Don't be rude, Pops," Molly scolded. "No matter what differences Hud and I have, he dropped everything to drive me over here so I could check on you."

Phineas let out a snort. "Well, aren't you a hero," he snapped, his eyes trained on him.

"Not in the slightest," Hud quipped. "But you already know that since I grew up in this town." Hud smirked at him, causing Phineas to laugh out loud.

"I can't argue with you on that," Phineas said, chuckling.

Molly clinked her spoon loudly against her saucer. "You never answered my question! What were you doing in the basement?"

Phineas turned to her. "If you must know, I was looking for some of your gran's letters and the Christmas ornaments. It's high time I put some up," he said. "I don't want folks to think I'm a Grinch."

Hudson wasn't prepared for the high-pitched squeal Molly let out. She got up from her seat and wrapped her arms around Phineas from behind. "Oh, that's so wonderful to hear. I know it hasn't been easy getting into the holiday spirit since we lost Gran."

Phineas ducked his head. "It's been difficult, but Eva would want me to celebrate the season."

"Since we're here, why don't we help you out?" Hud offered. "I can bring things up from the basement. I know a little something about decorating for the holidays." Due to his family's owning a tree farm, he'd been schooled at an early age on all things Christmas.

"I don't want to put you out," Phineas said. "Especially since I've already taken time out of your day."

"Just say yes, Pops. We're happy to help you," Molly said. She looked around the space. "Not to mention that this place really needs some holiday sparkle. The shop will be fine in Vinny and Estelle's hands for a couple hours."

Hudson was glad that Molly said it rather than him. Phineas was nothing if not prickly.

"Well, then, let's get this party started," Phineas said. "The Christmas boxes are to the right of the stairs under the overhead lighting."

"Okay then, I'll do the honors," Hudson said, standing up and making his way downstairs. After making a dozen or so trips, he'd completed the job.

"You sure have a lot of holiday decorations," he said, placing the last one down. His breathing was a bit choppy after getting this workout.

"Eva and I loved Christmas," Phineas said, a nostalgic smile lighting up his face. "I was blessed to spend almost sixty years with the love of my life. We enjoyed these collectibles. The last few years without her have left me feeling rudderless." He blinked away tears.

"You shared a true love story," Molly said, her eyes as

moist as her grandfather's. She gripped his hand, and the gesture spoke to the loving bond they shared.

"And this Christmas I'm going to put up every holiday ornament and trinket we ever collected. In her honor." Phineas puffed his chest out proudly.

Hudson placed his hand on the older man's shoulder. "Well then, let's bling this place out."

For the next hour, they decorated the interior of the house—snow globes, miniature trees, stars, wreaths, a vintage crèche. Then Molly and Hudson strung white and gold lights outside while Phineas watched from the doorway. The holiday lights were glistening and twinkling, and the look on Phineas's face made it all worthwhile.

"I think our job is done here," Molly announced as they put their coats on and said their goodbyes.

Phineas stuck out his hand to Hudson. "While I'll never agree with the way you served my Molly with legal papers, you're clearly a good man. It's not too late to take a different route."

As Hudson left Phineas's house, the older man's words settled over him, leaving him feeling conflicted. All this time he'd believed that laying claim to Humbled was the perfect way to uphold Lillian's legacy. But was it? If he ended up pursuing this matter in the courts, it would be extremely hurtful to Molly and her family. Even his beloved hometown would feel the aftershocks. His own family wouldn't be immune from criticism and censure either.

Could he really put everyone through it?

But he yearned to right a wrong in his Nana's honor. Only then would the gaping hole inside of him begin to heal. What kind of grandson would he be if he didn't follow through with his vow? That presented him with a huge dilemma.

He had no idea what he was going to do.

* * *

As Molly drove away from her grandfather's house, she could see the twinkling lights shimmering from the yard in her rearview window. The beautiful sight caused her to get choked up with emotion. Seeing Pops standing in the doorway waving goodbye to them had been heartwarming. She had seen a side of Hud that impressed her. Even though Pops had been prickly, Hud had shown him grace.

The snow still continued to fall as she drove the slick backroads toward town. Hud flipped on the radio to a station playing nonstop holiday music. Molly sang along while Hud hummed in sync to the songs.

"This one has always been my favorite," Molly said as the strains of 'Mary, Did You Know' played.

"That's my mom's favorite," Hud said, surprising her by singing along with her.

The atmosphere inside the truck was warm and cozy. Intimate even. Molly felt comfortable with Hud in a way that surprised her. She would never have believed that they would be on their way to being friends again. Or was she simply being too idealistic? A part of her was waiting for the other shoe to drop with Hud. She prayed he didn't have anything more up his sleeve.

When they arrived back in town, Main Street was fairly deserted. Humbled, along with the other shops, was closed. Lampposts were glowing silver and gold, giving some holiday flair. Serenity Peak's beauty was shimmering even in the darkness.

Molly parked in front of the shop, knowing Hud's vehicle was nearby. They both exited the truck and met up on the sidewalk.

"Will you be okay to get home?" Molly asked. He'd

been away from Alaskan roads for quite some time, and the snow hadn't let up.

"I'll be fine. It's only a fifteen minute or so ride, and it's like riding a bicycle. You never truly forget how to navigate these roads." He frowned. "What about you? Will you be all right?"

Molly's lips twitched. "I live upstairs, so I don't have far to go."

"Well, that's convenient. No wonder you beat me here every morning."

She met his gaze. "Hud, I can't thank you enough for everything."

"You don't have to thank me, Molly. I'm glad that I was there to help out. I had a good time."

"So did I," she said softly. Why was she feeling shy all of a sudden? She'd known this man all of her life. Maybe it was because he was reminding her of all the reasons she'd once fallen for him. His hazel eyes were magnificent. The woodsy scent that clung to him was inviting and warm.

"I'm relieved that Phineas warmed up to me because things were looking dicey for a bit," Hud said, scrunching up his face.

Molly laughed. She'd also been worried that Pops would be much harder on Hud than he'd been. He was loyal to her, to a fault. "Believe it or not, he's actually a big softie."

"Well, he sure is something else." Hud's features were creased with laughter.

Hud reached out and swept snowflakes away from her cheeks. His touch was gentle, almost like a caress. Something hummed and pulsed in the air between them. Despite the cold, Molly felt warmth spreading through her. What was going on with her? She hadn't felt this fluttery feeling in ages. Not since him.

She locked gazes with Hud. His eyes glimmered with something elusive that she couldn't quite put her finger on. His face was mere inches away from hers. Was Hud as confused as she was? It was just the two of them, the frigid night air and the snow falling gently from the sky.

Hud took a step toward her, closing the small distance between them. He began to lower his head, and she tilted her head upward in anticipation of the kiss.

Suddenly, a car came barreling down the street, spraying snow and sludge as it sped by, taking them both by surprise. Hudson took a step back away from her. "Well, I should get going," he said. "Night."

"Good night, Hud," Molly said, watching him walk away toward his vehicle.

The moment was lost, leaving her to wonder if they might have shared a kiss if the car hadn't interrupted their tender moment. Her thoughts were jumbled as she headed upstairs to her apartment. She and Hud had almost kissed. And although in the moment she'd been receptive, it would have been a mistake.

It would only serve to complicate things more. And Molly was already up to her elbows in complications.

Chapter Ten

Hud had wanted to kiss Molly the other night. He'd been so close to placing his lips against hers. The memory of that moment kept replaying in his head, over and over again. He'd sensed that Molly had wanted to kiss him too, although maybe that was wishful thinking on his part. It was a blessing in disguise that their tender moment had been interrupted.

There was way too much at stake with Humbled hanging in the balance. Kissing would only serve to complicate things. He hadn't wanted to think about the past, but Molly had a hold on him like no other. Falling for her all over again would be a mistake. Back then he'd fled town rather than give in to his feelings for her, ones that had tempted him to stay in Serenity Peak and give up all of his plans. Molly had the power to make him lose his head over her. And he needed to keep his eyes on the prize and focus on his goal.

Thirty days wasn't going to derail his plans. He had tossed and turned in bed the last few nights thinking about all the ways this situation could end. He couldn't see Molly caving in and giving him co-ownership of Humbled. On a good day, he wasn't sure she trusted him. Sure, they had moments where they got along and enjoyed a sweet chemistry, but under the surface there was a lot more going on. Mistrust. Their tangled history. Allegiances to their grandmothers.

Even during this most sacred time of the year, Hudson didn't totally believe that everything could be repaired between them. A spectacular Christmas blessing was what it would take, he imagined, for everything to be amicably settled.

The vibe between him and Molly the past few days had been detached, with neither one of them sliding back into the easy rapport they had enjoyed at Phineas's house. Tension hung in the air. Hudson thought maybe, like himself, Molly was trying to keep things professional between them. Although neither of them had brought it up, they both knew about their romantic past. The near kiss had brought those memories to the forefront.

He knew what kissing Molly was like. Her lips tasted like the sweetest nectar. Going down that path would be problematic for both of them. Hudson couldn't allow himself to get distracted by the most mesmerizing woman he'd ever known. Doing so would threaten everything he had come home to accomplish.

Focus! A lot was going on today at Humbled, and he needed to be present. The knitting circle was gathering this afternoon for their first social. They were all excited to see if any knitters showed up and if the event would be a success. Hudson felt slight pressure since it had been one of his ideas. The business could use a boost.

Lord, I know I keep asking You for favors, but I need another one. This place means a lot to me, and I really want this event to be successful. If You can swing this, I'd be really grateful.

He'd shown up this morning with gifts in hand. Although

the shop had been decorated with all sorts of Christmas adornments, there had been one thing missing. A Christmas tree. The Doherty tree farm had all types of trees of all shapes and sizes. He had found a stunning five-foot fir tree that would fit perfectly by the bay window.

"A little something to make the place sparkle even more," he'd said to Molly.

"This is amazing," Molly said. "I kept telling myself that I was going to pick one out, but time got away from me."

"Well, that's the good thing about my family owning a tree farm. I walk outside the house, and there are literally trees upon trees for the taking." Yet another thing he had missed about being home. Just the smell of the myriad of fresh Alaskan trees reminded him of his childhood.

"This is such a nice touch. Thanks, Hud." He could tell she was touched by the gesture.

For a moment she leaned toward him, and he thought she might hug him. Midway she corrected herself. He knew right away that she was worried about crossing lines. And he was too, although a hug from Molly would have been worth the risk.

Estelle stood a few feet away, watching them like a hawk. He had a feeling she had lots of thoughts about him and Molly.

Now, they were all at their stations, waiting to see if anyone showed up for the knitting circle meetup. One look at Molly and he knew that she, too, was feeling nervous. She'd been pacing around, trying to keep herself busy with customers on the floor. By twelve thirty, he noticed an uptick in customers, which wasn't unusual at this time of day. Time would tell if a crowd was gathering for the main event at one-thirty. They had cordoned off a section for the knitters and decorated the area for them. Although some had

RSVP'd, they were hoping that plenty more would simply show up to participate.

"Hey, Mrs. Locke," Hudson said when he spotted her entering the shop. She was carrying a large bag that read Knitting Rules and was overflowing with yarn and needles. He grinned at her. "I'm guessing you're here for the knitting circle."

"Please call me Jada," she said. "And I am definitely here to participate in the new group." She looked over at the designated area for the knitters.

"Is something wrong?" he asked. She was frowning as she surveyed the space.

"Yes, there is. I think you're going to have to make a bigger area," Jada said. "At least twice as big."

Out of the corner of his eye, Hudson saw a group of people entering the shop. When he turned toward them, he realized that they were all carrying knitting bags. Right on their heels, more customers streamed in.

Jada was right. They were definitely going to need a bigger space to gather.

Hudson excused himself and immediately sought out Molly.

"Molly, I'm going to expand the tables in the area we designated for the knitting circle," he told her. "Customers are coming in at a fast pace."

Molly looked around with wide eyes. "This is going better than I ever imagined." She turned toward him. "Your marketing expertise is really paying off."

"From your lips to God's ears," Hudson said, praying that the numbers continued to grow. It was funny how he now felt like a member of the team. This was a success for him as well.

"All hands on deck," Molly said. "Go take care of the

space, and I'll greet the knitters and direct them over to that area. Estelle's working the front counter. This place is really buzzing."

He could see the excitement shining in her eyes. She was mirroring his own feelings. Seeing an idea pay off was exhilarating. Knowing that he'd done something beneficial for the business made him feel as if his presence here was valuable. He wasn't simply the thorn in Molly's side. There was a feeling he couldn't shake that his Nana was looking down on him and smiling at all the work he was doing at Humbled. This was definitely something Hud could feel proud about.

Had he ever felt this ecstatic about any of his marketing campaigns in Boston? He didn't think so. There was something about working at Humbled that made him feel incredibly connected with his grandmother and the townsfolk. Molly too. There was something humbling about this job. He knew that he wasn't ever going to get rich in this line of work, but it didn't matter to him in the slightest. Feeling this way was a huge departure from the way he'd once felt. His original goals in Boston had been about gaining status and making the big bucks.

Ever since losing Nana, those aspirations had faded away. He barely recognized the man who had dreamed those dreams. And that was the thing. He could feel himself becoming a better man day by day. Maybe it was selfish of him to fight for co-ownership of Humbled even though he knew Molly was opposed to it, but at this point, letting go of it would be near impossible.

Business had been hopping today at Humbled. A feeling of pride threatened to burst from inside of her. The mood at the shop had been upbeat and festive. Community had been in full effect as customers gathered to knit, socialize and partake in drinks and snacks. There was something special about the vibe flowing through the space. She couldn't quite put her finger on it, but it seemed as if everything had come together in such wonderful symmetry, resulting in a beautiful event.

Molly had served the knitting group a special treat for their inaugural meet up. A spice cake that Gran had called "Love from Alaska." It had been her grandmother's signature holiday cake, always made with love. Barely a crumb was left by the group, who raved about the flavors and the fact that it was heart shaped. More than ever, Molly felt as if she were truly fulfilling Gran's heartfelt wishes—keeping Humbled as a gathering place for the Serenity Peak community. Fostering unity and togetherness. It meant even more during the Christmas season.

She had noticed that a few elders who rarely left their houses had shown up, and it made her chest tighten with emotion to see them here. Not everyone had daily contact with people. Some were lonely and in need of fellowship. That was what Molly wanted Humbled to represent.

At closing time, there were a few stragglers who didn't seem as if they wanted to leave. She had to admit that Hud had a nice way of announcing that the shop was closing without making customers feel as if they were being hustled out. More and more, Molly saw his value at Humbled while still disagreeing with his larger agenda. Although they were both making nice this month, she was curious as to what additional evidence he had in his possession to justify a lawsuit. There had been a reference to Lillian's journal, photographic evidence and personal documents but nothing more. Surely there had to be something more. He had sounded so certain regarding his position. Why?

At the Doherty home, Bert had alluded to the fact that Lillian had once sought to take the matter to court. That had been a bombshell reveal. Lillian and Eva had been the best of friends, and if they'd had a falling out, it must have been before Molly was born. Although it was possible she had been shielded from the issue by her family. Clearly they had patched up their relationship and resolved their differences.

Why can't Hud let this go?

Maybe her question was simply wishful thinking. Obviously Hud believed in his case. He was being sincere.

She watched as Hud put up the Closed sign and turned the lock on the front door. Vinny was cashing out the register in the bookstore. Estelle sat down on one of the stools by the counter and dramatically wiped her brow. "What a day this turned out to be. This is the first time I've sat down since I clocked in this morning."

Vinny came walking toward them. "Those knitting books you put on display were flying off the shelves," he said. "They've almost sold out."

Hud began clapping. "Outstanding." The look he sent Molly's way was full of admiration. It made her stomach feel fluttery.

Molly knew her grin was stretching from ear to ear. "I thought putting knitting books on display might be a nice cross promotion between the café and the bookstore."

"Great job, Molly," Estelle said. "You sure know your audience."

It was a good feeling being validated for making decisions that benefited Humbled. She had lots of ideas, but something always stopped her from putting them out there.

"Now that everyone's gone, let's have a toast," Molly suggested. She was practically walking on air at the moment. "I poured some sparkling apple cider into cups in the kitchen." She knew it was important to celebrate successes with her team. They had all earned a moment of revelry.

After they gathered in the kitchen, everyone raised a cup. "We all had a hand in today's successful event," Molly said, looking around her at Hud, Estelle and Vinny. "May we have many more days like this one. The holiday season has always been about community and fellowship. That was in abundance today. Cheers, everyone."

A chorus of cheers rang out, and they all clinked glasses.

After the celebration, Hud hung around to help Molly close up the shop. Each and every day he was learning new things about running the place. He was like a sponge, absorbing every little detail. She couldn't get over it. He was a big shot marketing executive in Boston, yet he was working alongside her at a modest shop in Alaska. Regardless of their differences, they had come together for a common purpose. His enthusiasm meant the world to her.

"I feel like jumping up and down," Molly said. "We had more business in one day than I've ever seen."

"And so many bought to-go bakery items as well as books. Cleaned us out," Hud noted. "When all is said and done, I think today's turnout showed how lucrative these events can be."

"I'm a believer," she said. "Who knew knitting would be such a hit?"

Hud tilted his head to the side. "I'm not surprised. It's becoming one of the biggest hobbies and not just for women."

Hud was right. The crowd had been a mix of men and women, young and old. Knitting appeared to be an equal opportunity pastime.

She nodded. "I noticed that! It's pretty cool."

"After what I witnessed today, I might take lessons myself," he said.

"I'll believe that when I see it," Molly said. Hud had never been one to sit still for long. She had a distinct memory of him fidgeting every day in class. "You used to get in trouble for not sitting still."

He made a face. "Yeah, I was diagnosed with ADHD back in college. So I had the double whammy of ADHD and dyslexia."

"Oh no. I'm sorry for bringing that up. I didn't know," she apologized. Open mouth, insert foot. She wished that she could take back her comment. Molly hoped it hadn't sounded judgmental.

"No worries. To be honest, getting diagnosed was one of the best things ever. Everything finally made sense." A painful expression crossed his face. "I could stop beating myself up for lack of focus."

She reached out and touched his arm, wanting to comfort him. His body radiated warmth, and she instantly realized her mistake. Touching Hud was a slippery slope. "I hate that you did that, especially for something that was outside of your control."

"It was my grandmother who insisted that I get tested. She'll always be watching over me." His voice sounded thick with emotion. She knew exactly how he felt. Both of their losses were relatively fresh. The pain was still sharp. The loss still caused an ache in her heart.

"We both have angels looking down on us," Molly said. "I could feel my gran's presence so strongly here today. She would have loved the knitting circle."

Something hummed and pulsed in the air between them, a connectivity that had been growing for weeks now. Seeing Hud's passion for Humbled had endeared him to her.

Hud leaned down and pressed his lips against hers. He reached out and placed his hands on the sides of her face, anchoring her to the kiss. This was everything she wanted, even though she hadn't been able to admit it to herself until this very moment. Molly began to kiss Hud back with equal measure, matching his intensity.

The kiss was full of tenderness, and she melted into him. His lips tasted like the sugar cookies she'd made earlier. She breathed in his scent—a mix of pine and something citrusy. At this moment, she felt so connected to him, the way he used to make her feel when they'd been together. She hadn't realized until now how much she'd missed it.

As they drew apart and the kiss ended, Molly felt the immediate loss of him. She didn't want the kiss to end, even though she knew they'd waded into dangerous waters. For a moment, they simply sat in the silence, avoiding saying a single word.

She was feeling a bit dazed. Molly almost felt like a child who'd known she shouldn't touch a hot stove lest she get burned. Yet she had done it anyway.

Too late. She couldn't turn back the clock. The threat of a lawsuit hung between them, serving as a huge distraction to anything more intimate developing between them.

"We shouldn't have done that," Molly said, biting her lip.

"I—I know," Hud said, stumbling over his words. He appeared just as shaken as she felt.

"We're colleagues. It's not a good idea for so many reasons." Between her past relationships with Hud and Will, Molly didn't have a great track record in the romance department.

"I'm sorry. It's all on me. I got carried away with the amazing day we had," Hud said. "I was acting on pure adrenaline."

"It's not just on you," Molly said. "We both know that

we…have a history. We've been down this road before. And it didn't end well."

Bam. She'd put it out there. The thing that neither one of them had mentioned even though it radiated between them like warmth from the sun. They had been seeing each other until he took off without a word of goodbye. To this day, Molly had never confronted him about his disappearing act.

Hud seemed crestfallen. "Molly, I never apologized for taking off like that."

"That was ages ago," Molly said. She was pretending as if it was nothing, when in reality it still hurt. She'd never truly gotten closure. "I got over it a long time ago," she fibbed.

"Really? Because I haven't." He swept his palm across her cheek. "I left because being with you was the only thing powerful enough to stop me from going to Boston. At the time, I thought my whole life was riding on that decision. As wrong as it was to leave like that, I knew that if I had to say goodbye to you, I wouldn't be able to go."

Tears sprang to her eyes. For so long, she'd wondered why he'd left. And now he was coming clean and telling her his truths. It meant a lot to her, but it was also causing old emotions to crash over her like a tsunami. Right on the heels of their kiss, she felt way too vulnerable at the moment to discuss this.

"I appreciate your honesty," she said. Even though it had taken him more than a decade to get the words out. She was being petty, but a part of her felt annoyed that he hadn't spoken up years ago.

"Are you all right?" Hud asked. "Talk to me, Molly. I know that I sprung that information on you."

She put on her best game face. "I'm fine, but it's been

a long day for both of us. Why don't you head home and I'll lock up."

"Are you sure?" Hud asked, searching her eyes.

"See you tomorrow. Night, Hud." She turned away from him and focused on making sure all the burners and appliances were turned off.

"Good night," he said. She heard the click of the back door closing. Only then did she let out the breath she'd been holding. His confession about the past had left her reeling. Why hadn't he simply told her how he was feeling? She would have understood and supported his plans. Instead he'd taken a torch to everything they had shared and made her believe he hadn't cared at all.

Despite knowing better, she and Hud had given in to the kiss this evening and their mutual attraction. It hadn't been a smart move, especially since they had been managing to put their differences aside to work together for a common good—Humbled.

What was I thinking?

It wasn't as if they were going to settle the issue of co-ownership and walk off into the sunset together. If they weren't able to come to an agreement, Hud was intent on taking the matter to the courts after the thirty days were up. The court fees alone would ruin her. She couldn't help but wonder if that was part of the plan.

No way! Her mind rejected the idea. There was no way Hud could be that calculating. He was a good person despite the fact that he was trying to assume ownership of something that wasn't his.

The bottom line was that she couldn't allow herself to give in to the feelings that had been stirred up by his return. Her focus needed to be on Humbled and retaining sole ownership. She had worked way too hard to allow Hud to just waltz back to town and take half of what was hers.

And she certainly wasn't going to let him burrow his way back into her heart. It had taken her a long time to recover from Hud the last time around.

Or maybe, she realized, she'd never truly gotten over him.

Chapter Eleven

If Hudson had thought for one minute that a single kiss and complete honesty would change things between him and Molly, he now realized he'd been mistaken. He was working a shift at Humbled and trying his best to decipher Molly's mood. Although he knew that the kiss complicated things, he didn't regret it for a single second. Unlike Molly, who'd acted as if they'd been caught robbing a bank. That, along with his transparency about the past, had clearly left her reeling.

Days had gone by and clearly she hadn't recovered. He had tried to lighten the mood between them with jokes, but Molly wasn't having any of it.

Tensions between them were as thick as pea soup. Just as the thought popped into his head, another memory wrapped around him and held on tight. Whenever he'd been sick as a kid, Nana had made him pea soup and sourdough bread. She had sprinkled parmesan cheese over the soup and made sure that there were generous chunks of ham in it. There was now an actual ache that wouldn't let up.

As happy as he felt to be back in Serenity Peak, it made his loss more painful. Maybe that was one of the reasons he'd stayed away for so long. In Boston he had been able to keep the memories at bay, but here in Alaska they surrounded him. And there was nothing he could do but go through it. He was praying to get to the other side, where he could fully accept the loss without allowing regrets to cloud the situation.

"What's the story between you two?" Estelle asked. She jerked her chin in Molly's direction as she vigorously wiped down a table.

Hudson shrugged. "I have no idea what you're talking about. That's my story, and I'm sticking to it."

Estelle stared him down. "Well, whatever it is, you better squash it. We have our holiday dating mixer tonight. It won't be beneficial if any participants pick up on negative vibes."

He held up his hands. "I agree, Estelle. I'm radiating nothing but love and light."

Estelle rolled her eyes before walking off. Clearly she knew something had gone down with him and Molly. She was a shrewd woman. How many other folks would detect that there was something going on? Estelle was right. Clearing the air with Molly before tonight's event would be wise.

Now he just had to find a way to thaw the ice with Molly. She was acting frostier than an Alaskan winter night.

Just after lunchtime, he found the perfect opportunity. She had been in the kitchen putting the finishing touches on a batch of petits fours for tonight's event. But now she was in the bookstore handling customers and stocking shelves. It was a bit quieter in the bookstore, and they wouldn't have a café full of customers listening in.

He just had to break down the wall she'd put up between them so they could get back to being friends. Was that what they'd been? At the moment, he actually had no idea. Friends didn't share kisses that were impossible to stop thinking about. Friends didn't show up in your dreams the way Molly had the last few nights.

Their path hadn't been straightforward. Childhood friends to something more than friends then frenemies before becoming coworkers slash friends. Maybe this was part of the problem. Perhaps Molly's head was beginning to spin trying to figure out where they stood with one another. And of course he'd complicated matters by trying to explain why he had left town so abruptly. He had wanted to get that weight off his chest so he could feel lighter, but Molly hadn't seemed better off with the knowledge.

Maybe in the future he should just keep his mouth shut. Making himself vulnerable never worked out for him. He hadn't been ready to tell her his truths before now. Hud figured that since they had grown closer it was the perfect time to be completely transparent.

"I brought you a peace offering," Hudson said as he approached, handing her a blueberry scone. Upbeat Christmas music was playing through the sound system, providing a joyful ambiance.

She was standing at the checkout desk, placing sale stickers on a stack of books. He had placed the scone on a little pink saucer and surrounded it with fresh berries and cream. As far as presentation went, he thought he deserved an A plus. For a moment, she just stared at him without saying a word.

"You took that from the cooling rack in the kitchen, didn't you?" Molly asked, sighing. "And I made them, so you're gifting me with something that's already mine."

He shrugged, feeling sheepish. "It's the thought that counts though, right?"

"Yeah, right," she snapped, sounding crabby.

"Okay, I know you're annoyed with me for many reasons, but at least give me some credit for knowing that you love scones. I could have chosen so many other treats to gift you with."

"Ha!" Molly said. "Since Christmas is rapidly approaching, I think someone needs to explain the concept of a gift to you." The corners of her mouth were twitching, and he knew she was softening up.

"Point taken," he replied. "I know things got complicated the other night, but—"

Molly's eyes widened, and she put her finger to her lips. She walked away and began looking amongst the shelves. A few minutes later she came back. "Just wanted to make sure that we were alone. These shelves have big ears."

"Understood," he said. Serenity Peak was a wonderful town, but it hadn't escaped his notice that gossip tended to fly on the wind. The last thing they needed was for a rumor to circulate that they were an item. "As I was saying, I know things got complicated, but I thought it was important that you heard the truth. Straight from my lips."

Molly reached for the scone and dipped it in the cream before taking a big bite. "I respect that, but it would have been better if you'd been straight with me at the time."

"In a perfect world, yes," he said, knowing he'd been in the wrong.

"You would have saved me a lot of heartache." Molly's words detonated like a bomb blast. *She had been heartbroken? Over him?*

"Molly, I'm sorry. I didn't know." He wished that he'd been aware of how much she'd been hurting. Would he have come home to console her? He didn't know for sure, but he would have tried to make things better.

"Of course you didn't. How could you? You took off to Boston without a single word, leaving me high and dry."

She was breathing heavily now, and he knew that he was in for it. "I'm not sure if you remember, but we had plans to go to the summer festival. You stood me up. It wasn't until the next day that your mother told me you'd left early for Boston.

"I even humiliated myself by asking her if you had left me a note or a message." She let out a brittle laugh. "And guess what? The joke was on me because you couldn't get out of Serenity Peak fast enough. I was the last thing on your mind."

"That's not true!" Hudson said. Molly wouldn't look at him. Instead she was focusing on a point in the distance. "That isn't true," he said again, this time louder.

"Shhh," Molly said. "They might hear you next door."

"I don't really care who hears me at the moment other than you," he told her.

Molly crossed her arms around her middle. At least now she was looking straight at him, even if she was glaring at him.

"Ten years ago I messed up. Badly. I was afraid, Molly. Too afraid to even talk to you and put my feelings out there. I've never really been any good at that."

"I never would have guessed," she said dryly.

"We always skirted around our feelings when we were together and left things unspoken," he said. "I knew that I was falling for you and that terrified me. I didn't have a single clue as to how you felt. I just knew that we were good together. You deserved a goodbye."

"Yes, I did," she said, her voice trembling.

"And bringing everything up right after we kissed was—"

"Stupid," Molly said, interrupting him.

He scowled at her. "You're not going to make this easy for me, are you?"

She grinned at him. "Nope, not for a single second. I've waited a long time to see you eat crow."

This was the Molly he'd grown up with. Sassy and full of spunk.

"Well, my timing was off," he admitted. "I should have realized it wasn't the right time or place. And for that I am very sorry."

"Apology accepted," Molly said in a quiet voice. "I do appreciate your vulnerability. It's not easy to peel back one's layers and admit fault."

He pressed his hand against his chest. "Gasp. Are you... giving me a compliment?"

She playfully swatted her hand at him.

"And another thing," he said, locking gazes with her. "This might fall into the category of TMI, but the one thing I'm not sorry about is the kiss we shared."

Molly's eyes widened and her cheeks flushed.

"Hud, I—" she began. A rustling sound in one of the aisles captured their attention.

"Is someone there?" Molly called out. Seconds later a woman with bright red hair and freckles came tiptoeing out, her arms full of books. "Brooks!"

"I'm so sorry, Molly," the woman said. "I heard the two of you talking and realized it was an intimate conversation, so I just wanted to hide out until the coast was clear."

"Got it," Molly said, clearly flustered that their entire conversation had been overheard.

"You must be Hud," Brooks said, sticking her hand out. "It's a pleasure to meet you."

"Likewise," Hudson said. He was meeting Brooks for

the first time. Apparently she'd moved to Serenity Peak in the years after his departure.

"I'm going to purchase these," Brooks said, dumping her armful of books on the counter.

"You've got a lot of great reading here," Hud said, picking up one of the books that had been a childhood favorite. *The Count of Monte Cristo*.

"Brooks is one of our best customers. She has great taste in books," Molly noted, smiling at the customer. Hudson didn't think Molly realized how disarming her smile was. It made him a little weak in the knees.

The woman seemed bashful, her face reddening at the compliment. "Books are great companions. They nurture the soul."

Molly let out a gasp. "That's beautiful. May I use that for my chalkboard quote?"

"I'd be honored," Brooks said. "I'm excited about the mixer tonight. It's been hard to meet people as a newbie in town."

Molly rung up and bagged the young woman's items then handed her back her credit card.

"We're going to make sure that you have a great time," Hudson promised. "Even if you don't make a love connection, you'll leave here tonight with a new batch of friends."

"I'd like that very much," Brooks said. "I'm grateful for the day I found this shop. It means the world to me."

After Brooks left, Molly looked at him and said, "Just when you think you're not making a difference in this world, someone shows you that you were dead wrong." Her voice was muffled, and she sounded sniffly.

"Are you crying?" Hud asked. *Uh oh*. Tears had always been his kryptonite.

"No," she said, rubbing at her eyes. "I'm just a little misty-eyed."

He went behind the checkout desk and put his arm around Molly, pulling her against his side. Her body relaxed against him. "That's understandable," Hudson said.

"It's nice when you get affirmation that you're doing something right," Molly said.

It had been a long time since he'd felt that way. But right now, because of Humbled, he prayed that he too was making a difference.

Music blared out of the Bluetooth speakers, filling the air with holiday songs. Molly tapped her foot to the rhythm as a feeling of contentment enveloped her. She was happy in a way that had seemed impossible the day Hud crashed into town. Back then she'd been afraid and angry. Now, she felt closer to him than she had ever imagined possible. Considering the fact that they were still disputing ownership of Humbled, it was a stunning development.

Hud had changed, she realized. He was more open and vulnerable. More willing to apologize and admit his mistakes. His sweet vibe with children and his willingness to always pitch in at the shop. Watching him with her grandfather had shown her his sensitive, caring side. She was drawn to him in a way she couldn't even make sense of. All Molly knew was that, despite her best intentions, he was tugging on her heartstrings. Even when she was annoyed with him, she couldn't stay mad for long. He was really starting to grow on her.

The way he smiled at her caused her stomach to do flip-flops. He could sure put on the charm when he wanted to. And she wasn't immune to it.

They had closed up the shop for a few hours in order to

set up for the singles mixer tonight. They were working fast and furiously trying to transform the space into a venue amenable to meet cutes. The tables had been rearranged to lend the meetups a more intimate vibe. Small batches of flowers and candles were being placed on every table. Molly had meticulously curated a lively and fun menu for the event.

Granted, a lot of folks already knew each other from having lived in town, but this evening represented new beginnings. Anything was possible.

"Jingle bell, jingle Bell, jingle bell rock," Hud sang as he set up the tables. Molly watched as he reached for Estelle's hand and twirled her around the makeshift dance floor. He looked dashing and goofy at the same time.

When people started to file in, Molly personally greeted everyone and handed out red and green ribbons that each person would use to show interest in a particular individual. There was also a big bowl of candy canes that would also come into play this evening. She had come up with the idea of arranging candy cane deliveries to participants from admirers. Each person could only submit one candy cane request. Although it would entail a lot of running around to deliver the candy canes, Molly thought it was a lovely Christmas gesture that folks would appreciate. And Vinny had graciously offered to deliver all the candy canes.

"Poppy! So great to see you here," Molly gushed as the beautiful doctor walked into Humbled. She was such a hardworking woman who didn't seem to enjoy much downtime.

Poppy was decked out in her holiday finery—a red silk blouse and a long green skirt. "I'm thrilled to be here. My resolution for the New Year is to get out more."

Molly winked at her. "And if you find a match in the process, all the better."

"We shall see," Poppy said, squeezing her hand before walking toward the throng of guests.

With the help of Estelle, Molly laid out the rest of the refreshments—petits fours, gingerbread cookies, pecan triangles, peppermint bark and a large charcuterie board. Hud had filled a punch bowl with eggnog, topping it off with nutmeg. She was praying everything went off without a single hitch. Ticket sales had been brisk for the event so she knew there would be a nice-sized crowd. Walk-ins were also welcome, providing they weren't at capacity.

Things were a bit hectic as the event got into high gear, but everyone seemed to be having a good time. She noticed people pairing off and having intense conversations. Between townsfolk and workers at Sugar Works, the venue was packed. Molly even noticed a few unfamiliar faces. She spotted Hud talking to the Locke twins from across the room. It was nice to see Hud reestablishing friendships with his childhood pals. He didn't even resemble the confrontational person who had shown up at Humbled a few weeks ago. Was this a Christmas transformation or what?

"Ho, ho, ho," a deep voice called out. "I've been watching all of you and making a nice and naughty list." Decked out in full Santa gear, he began dancing to the strains of "Santa Claus is Coming to Town." He was twirling around and really giving himself a workout.

When Santa turned in her direction, Molly let out a gasp. There was no mistaking the fact that it was Hud dressed up as the man in the red-and-white suit.

Molly burst out laughing. Hud hadn't told them that he was going to be doing this. He was cutting a rug and entertaining the guests in style. Soon, other people joined along, creating a little dance party. He danced his way over to her and held out his hand. Molly took it, reluctantly allowing him to whisk her onto the dance floor. She wasn't big on public dancing. She'd always felt a bit stiff and awkward as prying eyes looked on.

Hud seemed to understand. "Don't worry. I've got you," he whispered in her ear. "Just follow my lead." She nodded as Hud whirled her around the space. Molly felt secure in his arms, which wasn't a feeling she was used to. By the time the song ended, she was breathless. For the life of her, she didn't know if it was the fast-paced dancing or Hud himself.

"That wasn't too bad, was it?" He deposited her back where he'd found her. Before she could even respond to his question, he was back on the dance floor and engaging the patrons.

"I know he kind of crashed his way into working here," Vinny said in a low voice, "but I think he's been good for the place."

"I know what you mean, and I agree," she said. Just saying the words out loud caused something to shift inside her. Maybe it was the spirit of Christmas or the festive vibe flowing around them. All this time she'd been focused on holding on to Humbled, fearing that if she gave an inch, Hud would take over. That hadn't been the case at all, leaving her to wonder if she shouldn't reconsider her position. Perhaps being in a partnership with Hud wasn't the worst-case scenario. Revenue was up, and new ideas were in the works for the shop's growth.

But what if he takes off again? a voice echoed in her ear.

He'd explained his rationale about leaving, but it didn't mean he wouldn't do a disappearing act again if things took a wrong turn. What if Humbled had a downturn in business? What if something blew up between them? Would any setbacks cause him to leave town?

She didn't want to count on him. She didn't want to believe anything he said or promised. He'd fooled her once in the past and that still played in her mind like a constant refrain. Molly had been safer when she and Hud had been at each other's throats. At least then her guard had been up. She had been wary of him. But now he was proving that he was a good businessman with a flair for creative ideas. He cared about Humbled. That seemed genuine. And so did he. Hud had layers and he wasn't the same man who had hurt her in the past. But after all the years of nurturing Humbled, she just wasn't able to trust anyone else with her shop.

And her heart was also at stake. Because if he packed it all up and headed back to Boston, she couldn't run the risk of him taking her heart along with him

Chapter Twelve

After the successful singles event at the shop, Hudson felt he was on a roll. Not that all the credit went to him, but it was nice to have come up with two successful events back-to-back. He cared a lot about helping people make connections, and watching them enjoy themselves during the holiday season was uplifting. Playing Santa had been a whimsical gesture that had paid off big-time. Seeing Molly's eyes light up with merriment had been fulfilling. Being right in the thick of things made him feel as if he belonged. For someone who had always felt a little bit like the black sheep, this was a euphoric feeling.

He wasn't the only one basking in the successful evening. As they set up for the next morning's rush, Molly couldn't stop talking about the folks who'd paired up or appeared to have made a love connection.

"Did you see Brooks and Charlie?" Molly asked in a gushing tone. "They were so sweet together. They gave me all the warm and fuzzies."

Charlie Johnson was a childhood acquaintance, along with his sister, Destiny. Charlie had always been laid-back and kind. He was a good guy. And from what he'd seen, Brooks was a sweetheart. They did seem like a wonderful match.

"Don't get them married off just yet," Hudson teased. "Let them get to know each other first."

"If they do tie the knot, Humbled can cater the reception," Estelle added, chuckling.

Molly held up a finger. "Don't laugh. It could happen," she said. "With love, anything is possible."

Molly sounded like a true romantic at heart. It was something he hadn't really known about her. Not for the first time, he found himself wondering if she'd found love over the last decade. Had her own heart been touched?

"Now wouldn't that make a good story to go viral?" Hud asked. These days, he always had his marketing hat on when it came to the shop. "I can just see the headlines. Couple hosts wedding reception at the shop where they met at a dating mixer."

"Now who's getting ahead of themselves," Estelle said, shaking her head.

"I saw Poppy talking to the Locke brothers," Molly added, "although it's hard to tell if there were any sparks flying."

"More like friendship," Hudson noted. "I could tell by their body language. They all seemed very relaxed. There wasn't an ounce of romantic tension." He hadn't observed the type of tension that flared up whenever he was within a ten-mile radius of Molly.

"Well, it was another successful event," Molly said. "Our social media account is full of folks asking when the next mixer is going to be held." Molly was all smiles. "I'm pretty blown away."

He enjoyed seeing Molly happy. That was becoming more and more important to him with each day that went by. And it confused him because for so long he'd just wanted to come back home and lay claim to what had been taken from his beloved grandmother. Time was relentlessly ticking away. Before he and Molly knew it, thirty days would have elapsed.

And then what? he asked himself. *What am I going to do?*

Could he really proceed with a lawsuit? He couldn't imagine taking Molly to court, even though he might have no other choice. He felt as if he had boxed himself into a corner. As far as he could see, there wasn't an easy way out.

Sweet, beautiful Molly. His feelings for her were intensifying, yet he'd made a vow to Nana that he still needed to uphold. How could he choose between Molly's feelings and what he owed Nana? It was an impossible choice.

The more Hud saw Humbled flourish, the more he wanted his grandmother to get the credit she was due.

He wasn't sure God was still listening to him, but Hudson wanted to offer up a prayer.

Lord, I need You. All this time I thought that I knew what my end game was. But I don't know anything these days. I need Your wisdom so I can make a decision that honors Nana without hurting Molly.

Hudson was on duty in the bookstore. It was the perfect day to be away from the hectic pace of the café. He needed calm and quiet so he could think. He really enjoyed helping customers find new authors and their next favorite book.

"Can I help you find anything, Autumn?" Hudson asked the striking woman perusing the shelves. She had a toddler beside her in a stroller, who was sleeping peacefully. Estelle had filled him in on Autumn's return to Alaska and her reunion with her former love, Judah.

"Thanks, Hud. I'm actually looking for a few new books for River. We can only read *Goodnight Moon* so many times," she said, chuckling.

"Now that's a classic," he said, turning toward the shelf behind him and browsing the books. "Ahh, this is a good one," he said, holding up a kid's book, *Where the Wild Things Are*. "This was always my favorite, and it's still really popular."

"Oh, that is a good one," Autumn said. "Really vivid pictures. Do you have anything set in Alaska? I'd love to show him at an early age."

"You've got it," Hudson said, searching through the books for the one that instantly came to mind. He felt a surge of triumph when he found it. "Here you go. You can't go wrong with this one." Hudson handed Autumn the book.

"*Mama, Do You Love Me?* This looks amazing. River's going to love this one," Autumn said, flipping through the pages. The images were bright and colorful, depicting Alaskan culture and the bond between mother and child.

"These should keep River occupied," he said, looking down at the sweet-faced child. He looked just like his mom.

"They sure will," Autumn said, grinning. "I better pay for these books. He's going to wake up soon and want lunch."

"I'll do that now," he said, grabbing the books and heading over to the checkout desk. Hudson processed her order and slipped a colorful bookmark in the bag.

"Thanks so much, Hudson," Autumn said. "Welcome home."

"Nice to see you," Hud said with a wave as she exited the bookstore.

Life in Serenity Peak moved at a slower pace than Boston. So did the bookstore. And he was embracing it. Now he couldn't imagine ever going back to the hectic pace of his old marketing firm or spending all his days chained to a desk. This heartwarming shop had wrapped itself around his heart and left an indelible impression.

He found himself looking forward to special dates on the calendar so they could plan unique events for their customers. Rediscovering the books he'd grown up on was a huge plus of working on this side of the shop. *The Outsiders. Sherlock Holmes. The Call of the Wild.* He was reading again after he settled in for the night. Reading hadn't been a favorite pastime of his until he'd learned how to work through his dyslexia. He was becoming a regular bookworm at this stage in his life, leaning in to his childhood pastime. For many years in his twenties, he'd put reading on the back burner.

He quickly scanned the shelves in the mystery section, letting out a satisfied sound when he struck gold. An oldie but a goodie.

Molly stood in the bookstore's entryway studying him. "You sure left a smile on Autumn's face. She's raving about you."

"It was great to see her again. It's been a long time. And her son is adorable."

"River is a sweetheart. It's nice to see her and Judah so happy," Molly said.

It was comforting knowing that Autumn had managed to come home to Serenity Peak and find her happy ending. Maybe there was hope for him yet.

He had never been one to dream about settling down, but ever since returning to his hometown, Hudson had begun to picture it. Someone to walk through life with. The sort of love his grandparents had enjoyed. And maybe, a few kids running around calling him Papa. The images had nestled themselves into his mind, making him believe they were attainable dreams.

"What do you have there?" Molly asked as she walked over. "More Hardy Boys?"

"Nope. Agatha Christie. Working here is like taking a walk down memory lane." He held up the red-and-black cover. "*Death on the Nile* is a classic."

Molly began fiddling with her fingers. She broke eye contact with him.

"Is something wrong?" he asked. "You seem nervous."

"Hud, I need to tell you that Abel just called. He wanted to check with us to see how things are going."

"And what did you say?" Hudson asked. In his opinion, everything had been going smoothly. The expression on Molly's face wasn't giving him confidence that she felt the same way. "Molly?"

"I said things were going well, but he also wanted to know where things go from here. Honestly, I couldn't give him an answer to that question because I have no idea." She met his gaze. "Do you?"

"I wish that I did, Molly, but I don't. I'm hoping that I'll have a better answer soon." Hud's response hadn't moved the needle one way or the other.

Molly couldn't stop thinking about Abel's question as she got back to work at the cafe. The thirty-day period would be up before they knew it. And then what? Hud hadn't been able to tackle the question either. In her heart of hearts, she'd wanted him to say that he had decided not to pursue the lawsuit. But he hadn't said that, leaving her feeling disappointed.

What had she expected? The past few weeks had made her forget how intense he'd been initially about the lawsuit. Just because they hadn't discussed it didn't mean the issue was dead and buried. At this point, she needed to keep praying for an amicable resolution. Hud was someone she deeply cared about. Being at odds with him would never feel right.

Lord, help us find a way. I know You can move hearts and minds. Please allow me and Hud to find peace about this difficult situation.

After the shop closed for the day, Molly suggested that Hud, Estelle and Vinny enjoy a good old-fashioned teatime. When they all agreed, she set up a table for four with tea and treats. She loved the fact that her gran had purchased several three-tier stands that held finger sandwiches and baked goods. Molly chose an assortment of scones, mini croissants and muffins.

"What a way to end the day," Hud said as he surveyed the table. She had used gran's best teacups and saucers, along with her favorite linen.

Vinny rubbed his hands together as he sat down. "I love high tea."

"Me too," Estelle said. "It makes me feel fancy."

Molly did the honors and served the tea while inviting everyone to help themselves to the treats. They sipped their tea and ate in companionable silence for a few moments.

"So are we setting up a booth at the tree lighting tomorrow night?" Estelle asked, looking around the table.

How could Molly have forgotten about the tree lighting? With so much going on at Humbled and with Hud, the event had totally slipped her mind. Good thing she was fast on her feet.

"We could put up a little Humbled stand and sell hot drinks and some goodies," Molly suggested. "Not for the whole night, but maybe for an hour or so. That way we can still enjoy the evening after we make a few sales."

"Sounds like a plan," Estelle said, flashing a thumbs-up sign.

"I can work the stand for a little bit, but I've got a hot date for the tree lighting," Vinny told them, grinning. "I met her at the mixer." He picked up his teacup, held his pinky high in the air and took a long sip.

Molly, Estelle and Hud began to chuckle.

"Talk about seizing the moment," Hud said, heartily slapping him on the back.

"Everyone needs to love and be loved," Estelle said, staring pointedly at Molly.

What was going on with Estelle these days? Between her loaded glances and comments about her love life, Molly didn't know what to think.

Or was she simply being sensitive because Hud was sitting at the table? Was that why it felt so painfully awkward?

Maybe her friend was shining a spotlight on something she was afraid to examine. She and Hud needed to come to a resolution about Humbled. There was so much at stake, and it wasn't just the shop that was up in the air. Her feelings for Hud were growing by leaps and bounds and Molly didn't have a clue as to how to process any of it. But she couldn't continue to put her head in the sand. Maybe it was time to take some chances.

Chapter Thirteen

Hud looked out of his bedroom window, letting out a sigh as he watched the sunrise. The sky was putting on a fiery display, lit up with orange and yellow bursts of color. Snowcapped mountains loomed in the distance, providing a postcard perfect vista. He could get used to this view, he thought. For a lifetime. This Alaskan landscape was a part of who he was, imprinted on him like a tattoo. He couldn't imagine straying far from Serenity Peak ever again. This was home. Hudson knew that now.

He made his way downstairs, inhaling the delicious aroma of breakfast foods emanating from the kitchen. These days he was definitely getting spoiled with his mother making him big breakfasts and hearty dinners.

"Morning," he said as he entered the kitchen. Hudson pressed a kiss on his mother's cheek as she stood at the stove grilling sausages.

A chorus of good mornings greeted him. With the exception of his father, it was a full table. An early riser, his dad was probably already working the tree farm.

"Hud, we'll see you later on at the tree lighting?" his mother said as she placed a big plate of eggs, sausage and grits in front of him on the table. Hud began to dig in to his breakfast while avoiding the question. He didn't want to disappoint his mother, but he still didn't think he wanted to go. The event was too tied up with Nana in all of his memories.

"I can't wait," Theo shouted, raising his fist in the air.

"Inside voices," Anna scolded him. "No yelling at the table."

Theo glared at his sister. "You're not the boss of me."

"That's true," their mother said, "but she's right. You were being impolite."

Hudson watched as his little brother rolled his eyes without his mother noticing. He leaned over and said in a low voice, "Mind your manners."

"Okay," Theo said in a meek tone.

Gramps clapped Hudson on the back. "That's what he needs. An older brother to set him straight."

"Hey!" Drew protested. "What am I? Chopped liver?"

The entire table burst into laughter at Drew's reaction. These, Hudson thought, were the moments he'd missed the most. Gathering around the table to share a meal as a family had always led to lighter moments like this one. No one knew him or loved him the way his family did. He really needed to tell them that he wasn't going back to his life in Boston. Gramps had already suspected the truth, but he needed to come clean. They were checking in with him every day about the goings on at Humbled and to check in on the status of the lawsuit. Yet, he still wasn't being truthful about his life. As it was, he was walking around with this weight on his shoulders. He didn't want any more lies.

"I have a little announcement," he said, drawing everyone's attention to him. Hudson cleared his throat. "I won't be going back to Boston after Christmas. I've decided that Serenity Peak is where I belong."

A hushed silence greeted his announcement until his mother let out a shout of joy. "Oh, my goodness," Leticia said. "All of my prayers have been answered." Tears pooled in her eyes, and she dabbed them away with her napkin.

"You said no shouting," Theo said, laughing. He leaned over and hugged Hudson just as Anna jumped up from her seat and enveloped him in an embrace.

"I'm so happy," Anna said, holding on tight.

Drew reached over and clapped him on the back, smiling broadly.

"You've made us all very happy," Gramps said. His voice was laced with emotion, and Hudson suspected that he was fighting back tears.

"Okay, enough mushiness," Hudson said. He also was blinking back tears. His family's reaction to the news that he was going to be a permanent resident of Serenity Peak was heartwarming. All the roads he'd been traveling for the last decade led right here to his family's table. Surrounded by love.

After breakfast, he headed into town with a full belly and an even fuller heart. Things were all lining up perfectly. Everyone had welcomed him back home with open arms. He was being accepted by the townsfolk, Molly and his coworkers. Making a life here almost felt seamless. He knew that there was still the huge issue of Humbled hanging over him, but his gut was telling him that everything was going to work out.

But how? a voice nagged at him. The reality was that someone would have to back down. Him or Molly. As much as he cared for Molly, Hudson couldn't see himself throwing in the towel. Doing so would be betraying his grandmother. In a perfect world, Molly would realize that Lillian deserved recognition and status as a cofounder of the shop. Anything less would feel like a failure, and he'd already let down his Nana. He couldn't bear to do it again.

A verse from Isaiah 41:10 came to mind. *Fear thou not; for I am with thee: be not dismayed; for I am thy God: I will strengthen thee; yea, I will help thee; yea, I will uphold thee with the right hand of my righteousness.*

He was learning to let his faith be stronger than his fear. Trust in the Lord. There was comfort in knowing that he wasn't alone. Despite the uncertainty of his situation, Hudson was choosing to believe that He would make a way for him. And Molly. Whatever happened, he needed for Molly to be okay. The thought of her having one moment of pain gutted him.

When he arrived at the shop, there was a vibe of excitement in the air. As soon as customers began filing in, the chatter was focused on the tree lighting ceremony. He'd almost forgotten what a big deal it was, but everyone—Molly, his family and the customers—were effusive with joy about the event.

Thad Josephs, one of their regular customers and his former teacher, came into the shop with his service dog, Lottie. Thad couldn't stop talking about the ceremony. Having lost his wife a few years ago, Hudson knew the holidays might be difficult. He imagined that big events brightened up the season for him.

"You're a big fan of tonight's event, aren't you?" Hudson asked the older man.

"Me and Lottie have been looking forward to it all season, haven't we, girl?" Thad asked the sweet Labrador retriever. "It's a reminder that none of us is alone in this world. We're all connected by threads that link us together," Thad said.

"I've never thought about it that way," Hudson said as he handed him his gingerbread latte. As far as he could tell, these holiday lattes were the drinks of the season. This was the fifth one he'd made this morning.

Thad grinned at him. "Good to know that I can still teach you a few things."

This was the beauty of a small town, he thought as Thad walked off with his latte and Lottie.

Hudson needed to tell Molly that he wasn't going to make the ceremony tonight. He didn't want her to expect him to show up and then think he was a no-show. He found a quiet moment after the lunch rush to tell her the news.

"If it isn't the gingerbread latte king of Serenity Peak," Molly teased as he walked up. Her eyes twinkled, and she seemed upbeat. He hated to be the one to bring her down, but he'd waited long enough to tell her.

"I'm not sure that I'll attend the tree lighting tonight," Hudson told her. He felt a bit guilty about his decision, but in his mind, the event was tied up with his grandmother. It would be painful to soak it all in with her being gone.

"What? This is the town's big event before Christmas. We close up the shop early and everything so we can all attend." Molly's disappointment was palpable. "Don't you remember how much fun it is?"

How could he put into words how he felt? The tree lighting event had been Nana's favorite town tradition. She loved gathering with her loved ones and the townsfolk to celebrate the joyful season of Christmas.

"This is what life's all about. Loving one another as He loves us."

Her voice was so strong in his mind that for a single second he allowed himself to forget that she was gone. It seemed as if she was standing right beside him.

Only she wasn't. And his heart ached with missing her. Not being able to say goodbye was still wreaking havoc on him. On days like this, he didn't think he would ever get past it. Even visiting her grave hadn't helped his healing.

"I'm not sure that I'm ready," he admitted. "My strongest memories of the tree lighting ceremony include my grandmother. I don't think we ever attended a single one without her."

"Oh, Hud. It's still so fresh, isn't it? Being back in Serenity Peak means you're experiencing a lot of firsts without Lillian."

Molly was spot on. It made him feel good that she understood where he was coming from. She wasn't just offering platitudes.

"Yeah, and sometimes for brief moments I forget she's gone, and then it hits me like a tidal wave that we lost her." The words slipped out of his mouth, surprising him. He wasn't used to baring his soul to people. But talking to Molly was different, he realized. She was different. She wasn't the type of person to judge or look down on him. Molly was a soft place to fall. He hadn't known many women like her. She was a rare gem.

"Someone once told me that grief is like a rushing river. When we least expect it, the feelings of loss can overwhelm us. It's not unusual to grapple with how to handle these big emotions," she told him.

Molly's words were spot on again. Clearly, she understood the road he was walking down.

"We're in this together," Molly said, grasping his hand in hers. "I'm grieving too. But I've learned that time is a wonderful healing balm. And sometimes being around people is the best remedy."

"I know you're still grieving Eva," he said. Sometimes he forgot that he wasn't the only one mourning a loss. Molly seemed to be navigating her way through grief in a much better way than himself. But maybe she was right. Time would help him heal.

"To be honest, I think I'll be grieving her for rest of my life," Molly admitted. "But everyone keeps saying that time is the great equalizer. It won't erase our grief, but the pain won't be as sharp."

"I keep reminding myself that whatever I'm feeling, Gramps is probably going through something way more intense. He was married to my grandmother for almost sixty years." Once again, guilt pierced his insides. Since his return, he'd been avoiding intimate conversations with Gramps and his parents. He should be asking them how they were doing and checking in on them. Despite his strained relationship with his father, he cared about him. He prayed daily that they would bridge the divide between them.

"Same with Phineas. He's had to learn how to live without his other half," she said, shuddering. "That's the downside of loving people. We lose them."

"But if you asked Gramps, he'd do it a thousand times over again," Hudson said. "He once told me it was the single bravest thing he had ever done. Choosing love."

Those words had stayed with him, making him wonder if he would ever find a love everlasting. If he were ever so blessed, he would cherish it.

"No pressure either way about the tree lighting ceremony," she assured him. "But I would love to hang out with you in a setting outside of the shop. I think it could be fun."

That definitely sounded appealing to him. So much of their relationship had been about Humbled and their tangled past rather than what they were building in the present. Yet, it was still confusing. Did he mean something to her? Or was he just someone she'd been forced to make peace with? He needed answers. If she felt even a small portion of how he felt, Hudson would consider that a win.

"Molly. What are we doing here?" Hud asked. Maybe she could put things in perspective for him. Save him from making a fool of himself if she wasn't interested.

Molly didn't even have to ask him what he meant. The push and pull of their attraction had been building for weeks, leading to the tender kiss they'd shared and an increased sense of intimacy between them. They both knew it.

"I don't know, Hud," she responded. "I've been asking myself that very same question. But I know that I like spending time with you. And for now, that's enough."

After closing up Humbled for the day, Molly quickly changed into a festive red-and-green outfit. Tonight's festivities called for an epic holiday outfit. The more sparkly the better. She was disappointed that she most likely wouldn't see Hud tonight at the ceremony. Of course she completely understood his situation, but she really had been looking forward to spending some downtime with him.

She always looked forward to seeing Hud, whether at the shop or bumping into him while running errands in town. Without even realizing it, she'd come to depend on him being around. He made everything better with his sense of humor and dependability. She loved the way he always got up and tried again after failing the first time. And when he smiled at her it seemed as if the world stopped spinning. On several occasions she had almost gotten lost in the depths of his hazel eyes.

Molly let out a groan. It didn't take a genius to figure out that she had it bad for Hud. And she knew he had feelings for her as well. That was why he'd asked her earlier what they were doing. Hud knew as she did, especially after the kiss they'd shared, that something intense was brewing between them. But, as they both realized, it was complicated.

That didn't mean they shouldn't lean into it. Take a leap of faith.

At six o'clock Molly was at the town green, bundled up in a thick parka, a warm knit cap and her coziest winter boots. Vinny was already there, manning the Humbled stand. Even though they were only serving hot cocoa and a limited amount of baked goods, there was already a line. Molly jumped in and began helping him with the orders. They got the line in control just as Estelle arrived.

"Sorry I'm late," she said. "It's so cold my truck needed a jump start." She also was decked out in all her festive green-and-red gear. She was wearing a pair of reindeer antlers on top of her hat and dangly candy cane earrings.

"We're just glad you're here," Molly said, giving her a hug.

"Looks like Hud's a no-show," Vinny said. "He didn't seem that enthused about tonight when we were discussing it."

"He told me earlier he might not make it," Molly said, letting out a sigh. "Events like this one can be difficult when you've suffered a loss."

"That's totally understandable. Lillian was a wonderful woman," Vinny said. "She used to order a chai tea and a croissant every single time she came by."

"And her money was never any good at Humbled," Estelle added. "Lillian made it clear that she had VIP status at the shop."

Estelle's recollection brought a smile to Molly's face. Eva and Lillian's friendship had been epic. She had no memories of them ever falling out over the shop. Whatever bumps in the road they'd experienced, it had all blown over. They'd made up and repaired their friendship. In an ironic twist, they had passed away within six months of one another. Their friendship had truly been from the cradle to the grave.

Molly glanced at the time. Vinny had just left to meet up with his date. Had she really already been here for a half hour? Time seemed to be whizzing by. She was still holding out hope that Hud would show up before the tree lighting began. Even though it wasn't likely, Molly still found herself praying for him to surprise her.

"Looking at your watch every five seconds won't make Hud show up." Estelle sent her a knowing look.

She began to bluster. "I—I'm not—" she said before stopping herself. What was the point in pretending? Estelle was her coworker and a close friend. Molly sensed she'd witnessed a few moments between her and Hud that had left her wondering.

"You're right," she said. Just saying the words out loud made her stand a little taller. What was the point of hiding how she felt? Estelle was one of her closest friends, as well as one of the most loyal. She didn't have to worry about her running her mouth.

Estelle winked at her. "I totally get the appeal. He's tall and handsome…and kind. He might just be a keeper."

"Yep," Molly said. "What can I say? Hud is totally swoonworthy."

"So go for it," Estelle urged. "You've got nothing to lose."

"Well, that's not exactly true. He could still sue me," she muttered. Despite her feelings, the thought was sobering.

"I can't see Hud doing that," Estelle said. "What's that saying? All bark and no bite?"

Molly pulled her knit cap down to cover her ears from

the biting cold. "Things are a bit muddled between us at the moment. I'm not sure we'll ever get to the keeper stage."

"Don't do that, Molly. Give it a fighting chance," Estelle urged. "Someone's ears must be burning," she said, looking at a point in the distance.

Molly followed her gaze. Hud was walking onto the town green, hand in hand with Theo. Overjoyed. That was how she was feeling right now. She'd almost given up on the idea of him showing up, yet here he was. Her heart began to thump wildly, and her pulse skittered. What was wrong with her?

Then it hit her like a ton of bricks falling on her head. She hadn't realized until this very moment that she was falling in love with him. She could feel it in every fiber of her being, right down to her toes. And it terrified her because it felt like she was walking a high wire without a safety net.

Chapter Fourteen

"Molly!" Theo called out as he raced toward her. She opened her arms wide, and he flew right into them. She hugged him tightly, realizing he resembled a pint-size version of Hud. And he was just as charming as his big brother. He probably had the girls in his class wrapped around his little finger the same way Hud had when he was Theo's age.

"It's great to see the two of you," Molly said, looking over at Hud.

"We wouldn't have missed it for the world," Hud said, smiling at her. She didn't know why he'd changed his mind, but she was over the moon about it.

"Can I go join my friends?" Theo asked. "They're over there by the pizza truck."

"That's fine," Hud said, "but don't wander too far. Okay?"

"Promise," Theo said as he ran toward the group of kids.

"So, what changed your mind about tonight?" Molly asked him. She had to remind herself to play it cool despite the wild thumping of her heart. Standing so close to Hud was doing strange things to her equilibrium.

"Well, Theo was twisting my arm, which can be pretty painful," he said, wrinkling his nose. "Not to mention that a beautiful woman reminded me earlier that being around people can be a great balm for grief."

Beautiful? Molly couldn't think of the last time a man had called her beautiful. Her cheeks warmed at the compliment. She didn't know how to respond. For most of her life, she'd considered herself a plain Jane.

"You do know that you're beautiful, don't you?" Hud asked, frowning at her. He was staring at her so intensely, as if he could see straight through her.

She shifted uncomfortably from one foot to the other. Best to tell the truth. "No, Hud. I've never thought of myself that way." Growing up as the best friend of the prettiest girl in town had always made her feel less than. It wasn't Skye's fault by any means, but she had always been hailed as the town beauty, not Molly. And until now, looks had never been her focus. But being considered beautiful by Hud was all kinds of wonderful. It made her feel all tingly inside.

A look of outrage was stamped on his face. He took a step closer to her. So close she could see the breath vapor coming from his mouth. Hud reached out and swept his gloved hand across her cheek. Much to her surprise, he didn't seem to care who saw him make the affectionate gesture.

"Molly!" Suddenly Skye was standing there, looking back and forth between her and Hud. Molly inwardly groaned. The look on her best friend's face was one of annoyance. She knew Skye well enough to realize this wasn't going to be pretty.

"Skye," she said, greeting her warmly with a hug. Her best friend smelled like freshly baked sugar cookies.

"It's been a long time, Skye," Hud said, sounding friendly.

"Hud." Skye's one-word response spoke volumes. Her

best friend wasn't about to exchange pleasantries with him. Her loyalty to Molly meant that she was still holding a grudge against him for showing up in Serenity Peak with legal papers in hand. Molly felt a bit guilty. She should have reached out to Skye and told her that Hud had managed to turn her opinion of him around with his hard work and positive attitude.

A tense silence stretched out until Hud said, "I'm going to go say hi to Brody. I'll be back."

"You made that awkward," Molly said, chiding her friend after Hud was out of hearing range.

Skye tugged on Molly's arm and pulled her to the side, leaving Estelle to man the table.

"Why are you protecting him?" Her friend's features were creased with concern. "What's going on between you and Hud?"

"What do you mean?" Molly asked, stalling for time to come up with an answer.

"Molly Truitt! We've been best friends since the cradle. I know you inside and out. Something is brewing between the two of you." She nudged Molly with her elbow. "And judging by the way he was touching your cheek it's something romantic!"

Molly almost laughed out loud at her friend's dramatic delivery. She had been this way since they were small. "Will you give me a hard time if I say yes?"

"No," Skye said, "but I'll just remind you of what happened the first go round with Hud. He hurt you."

"You don't need to remind me, Skye. I was there."

"And you still think it's a good idea to give him another shot?" Skye asked, her eyes widening.

"Hud's changed. He's definitely not the same person who left Serenity Peak without a word of goodbye." She stood up a little taller, buoyed by her belief in Hud. "Matter of fact, that was a boy. This Hud is a man. And he means a lot to me." Her voice cracked with emotion.

Skye was listening intently. Molly knew that she was taking her words to heart. She prayed her best friend would understand.

"I get lonely sometimes," Molly admitted. "It hasn't been easy watching all of my friends fall in love and settle down. I want that too. I want someone to walk through life with at my side."

"Oh, Molly," Skye said, "you deserve all the happiness the world has to offer. You've always stood by my side through thick and thin. If you think that you can find joy with Hud, I fully support you."

The two women leaned in for a tight embrace. Molly could feel Skye's love infused in the hug. This was true friendship—understanding and compassion without judgment.

"I don't know exactly what this is between me and Hud, but it feels special," she admitted. "It's not like anything I've ever known before." Even talking about her emotions made her feel vulnerable, but Skye was a trusted friend and a great sounding board. This was all so new to her. And she still had no idea if Hud's feelings mirrored her own.

Skye wiped away tears with her mittened hand. "Oh, Molly, if you like him then so do I. Team Hud. Oh my gosh. If you mix Hud and Molly, you get Holly." She let out a little squeal.

Molly couldn't help but giggle at her friend's over-the-top excitement. "We're not a couple yet, Skye." She had to admit the moniker *Holly* was brilliant.

"But you've kissed him, right? I could tell by the way you were talking with him that there's loads of chemistry."

"We did kiss," she said as a memory of their smooch popped into her mind. Molly instantly regretted telling Skye when she emitted another ear-splitting screech. This time, several townsfolk turned in their direction to see what was going on.

Looking sheepish, Skye covered her mouth.

"Way to play it cool," Molly said, shaking her head.

Skye's tinkling laughter rang out. "You know me. I struggle to behave."

Just then Skye's husband Ryan walked up carrying their toddler, Lula, on his hip while a smaller baby was in a baby sling on his chest.

"Mama," Lula said as she laid eyes on Skye. The cherub-cheeked cutie was adorable.

"Just checking to make sure you ladies are all right. I heard some blood-curling screams emanating from this direction," he teased. Skye opened her arms and took Lula from her husband, placing a kiss on her temple.

Just watching Skye holding her daughter in her arms with Ryan standing beside her caused a yearning inside of Molly that wouldn't subside. *This is what I want for myself*, she realized. Abiding love and a family of her own.

"Why don't you take a picture of Molly? It'll last longer," Brody quipped. His deep brown eyes were twinkling, and little creases had formed around the sides of his mouth. He'd always had a jovial sense of humor that endeared him to everyone in Serenity Peak. Hudson had missed his friend's humorous comments and laidback vibe.

Caden joined in on the laughter. "Who knew, Hud? You've got a thing for Molly, don't you?"

"So much for just being friends," Brody said. "I told you

that anything can happen during the holiday season. I don't want to say I told you so, but… I told you so."

"I see neither of you have changed one bit," Hudson said, chuckling along with them. "Let's just say Molly has been one of the best things about coming home."

The brothers each let out an oohing sound. Hud didn't mind the ribbing. These guys were two of his oldest friends, and he knew their intentions were good. At the moment he didn't care who knew that he was crushing on Molly.

"No, seriously, Hud. We approve," Brody said. "Molly's the real deal."

"She is," Hudson agreed. "Speaking of which, I should head back to the stand in case she needs my help."

"See you later," the brothers said as they headed in the direction of the tree.

By the time Hudson circled back to the Humbled stand, it was just Molly packing up items.

"Anything I can do to help?" he offered. From the looks of things, there wasn't much left to do.

"No, but thanks for asking. I told Vinny and Estelle that they could go enjoy themselves. We sold out so there wasn't much to pack up," Molly said. "I'm done," she announced. "And now I can enjoy this wonderful evening."

"Another success for Humbled. What's next? The Super Bowl?" he teased.

"Now wouldn't that be something?" She crossed her hands prayerfully. "I like to dream big. I've always considered Humbled as the little shop that could. It's always exceeding my wildest dreams."

He liked the way Molly wasn't afraid to dream big. Somewhere along the way, he'd forgotten to do that for himself. She didn't realize it, but Molly was encouraging him to do just that. For so long he had been following the wrong path and chasing a chaotic lifestyle that hadn't suited him. Now, he was free to focus on things that brought him joy.

An announcement came from the direction of the stage, alerting them to the fact that the tree lighting ceremony would be beginning in ten minutes.

"Shall we?" he asked, extending his arm so Molly could loop hers through it.

"People will talk," Molly said, questions lurking in her eyes.

"Let them," Hud said. "Life's too short to worry about what people might say. My Nana taught me that. What better way to honor her than to live out her beliefs?"

Isn't that why he had decided to come back home? To honor his grandmother. He was discovering that there wasn't only one way to accomplish his goal.

"I like the sound of that," Molly said. A smile played around her lips. "Although I'm sure we'll be deluged with questions, ones we might not have answers to." She bit her lip. He knew that she was thinking about their discussion from the other day, when neither one of them could put their relationship into words.

Now was the time to speak his truth.

"Molly, if anyone asks, I'm going to tell them that you make me smile every time we're together. I laugh more. My heart feels lighter. I love brainstorming ideas with you and the way you always respond with enthusiasm and support." He looked into her eyes, and what he saw there emboldened him. "The other day I asked you what was going on with us, but I knew. You make me feel things I haven't felt in a very long time. I want you in my life, no matter how things shake out with Humbled."

He could see she was overwhelmed by his words. A sheen of tears pooled in her eyes. "No one has ever said that to me, Hud. Not ever. And in case you're wondering, I want you in my life as well. And not just at the shop as my coworker." She squeezed his hand. "As something infinitely more personal."

His chest swelled upon hearing her words. They still had mountains to climb, but he was praying their relationship could withstand any upheaval. He tried to quiet the negative voice inside his head warning him not to get too comfortable with Molly.

As they walked toward the tree, he couldn't ignore the curious looks in their direction. The glances didn't make him feel awkward or as if he were being regarded under a microscope. These folks cared about both of them, and if there was something developing between him and Molly, they'd want to know about it. No doubt they would be all in their business, but they would also cheer them on. That was how the Serenity Peak community operated.

Gramps gave him a thumbs-up sign as they drew closer. The rest of his family was standing there as well, including Theo, who was still with his pals. Looking around the area gave him a warm feeling. There were so many townsfolk in attendance who had played a role in his development. Friends. Teachers. Church members. It seemed to Hudson as if the entire town had shown up for the celebration. They were all here, dressed in their holiday finery and spreading good cheer. His family's tree was majestic—tall, full and stately. A burst of pride flared in his chest just knowing that his family had cultivated this stunning Fraser fir. It stood as a beacon of hope and inspiration.

Serenity Peak's mayor, Abilene Jenkins, stood at the podium trying to hush the crowd so she could speak. Abilene drew her fingers together and let out a sharp, high-pitched whistle into the microphone. Within moments the crowd quieted down.

"Now that's how you quiet a crowd," Hudson said, whispering in Molly's ear.

"Absolutely," Molly said. "She really knows how to command an audience."

"Thank you everyone," Abilene said. "We're gathering here this evening for the town's penultimate holiday event. Our annual tree lighting ceremony."

Everyone began to cheer enthusiastically.

"Christmas is a time to celebrate the birth of Christ and to strengthen our ties to our brethren," the mayor continued. "And God said, 'Let there be light.'" Abilene flipped a switch, and the tree was lit up in spectacular fashion from the shining star on the top to the lowest hanging branches.

Hudson turned toward Molly. Her face was lit up by the glow emanating from the tree. She was radiant. Her skin glistened, and she had a smile that stretched across her face. Once again he linked his hands with hers. At the moment there was no place he'd rather be than right here in the thick of things with Molly at his side. These were the moments he would cherish for the rest of his days. So far he'd been able to handle the tidal wave of loss.

"And now," Abilene said, "we're going to commemorate those we've lost in our community over the past few years. The ones who are no longer here. May their lights continue to shine as we hold them near and dear to our hearts. Never to be forgotten."

As she began to list the names, Hud felt sweat breaking out on his forehead. His head began to pound. What was going on? Up till this point, he'd been fine.

"Hud, are you okay?" Molly whispered, leaning into him.

His hand went slack, and he let go of hers. He turned in

his grandfather's direction. Bert was swatting at his eyes with a handkerchief.

I let him down. I let them all down. He hadn't been around to help them grieve. Even now he felt helpless to help Gramps.

"Lillian Doherty." Her name rang out in the stillness. He had somehow forgotten this poignant portion of the ceremony. His chest felt tight the moment her name was read. His hands were shaking. Of all the moments to fall apart. He couldn't bear the thought of Molly thinking that he was weak, but if he stayed, Hudson feared he would come apart at the seams.

Deep breaths, he told himself. Try as he might, this tactic wasn't working for him. He felt as if a sharp object was lodged in his chest. Was he having a panic attack?

"I—I can't do this, Molly. I'm sorry," he said as he turned and beat a fast path away from the crowd. With every step he took away from the town green, he considered himself more of a failure. He couldn't even face this moment without breaking down.

Just when Hudson thought that he was getting stronger and more grounded in his new life, he was realizing that he was just as broken as he'd been three years ago.

Chapter Fifteen

The moment Hud took off, Molly racked her brain trying to figure out what had happened. So far it had been a beautiful evening, full of fun and fellowship. Hud's entire demeanor had shifted the moment the ceremony began. She didn't hesitate to race after him. Although she did her best to keep up with his strides, Hud outpaced her. It was only when she began lightly jogging that she made any headway.

All of a sudden, he stopped and bent over at the waist as if catching his breath.

"Hud. Are you all right?" Molly asked. She placed her hand on his arm, and he stiffened up. "What's going on?"

"The memories kind of swept me under," he admitted. "And when the names were being read, I just started feeling sick to my stomach and very shaky."

"Well, this is the first time you've had to face the loss in a big public setting," Molly reminded him. Up to this point, Hud had been able to shove it down into a little black hole. It would have been impossible to do that tonight

"I didn't get to say goodbye," Hud said, pain infused in his voice. "While she was lying in a hospital bed taking her last breath, I was in Boston working at a job I hated." He sank down onto a bench and held his head in his hands.

Whoa. Her whole perception about Hud living a spectacular life away from Serenity Peak had just been blown to smithereens. She'd been of the belief that he loved his job. Wasn't that why he'd stayed away for so long?

"I wasn't there for her," Hud said, sounding agonized.

"I'm so sorry. I know this must feel unresolved. Not being able to be there by her side must have been devastating." As someone who'd had the privilege of being at her own gran's hospital bed as she drew her last breath, Molly commiserated with him. A part of her felt guilty. She had encouraged him to attend the ceremony tonight despite his reservations. She hadn't realized that it would trigger so many feelings of guilt and loss.

"What can I do?" she asked. Molly knew in all likelihood that the only thing she could do was be by his side supporting him. And she intended to do just that for as long as he needed her.

Hud shrugged. "Just being here lets me know I'm not alone."

She sat down next to him and placed her arm around him. "You're not alone, Hud. Not in any way, shape or form. This town adores you."

"If only I'd known how ill she was. She didn't want anyone to know she had a heart problem. The virus further weakened her heart, which caused a medical crisis." He clenched his teeth. "Coming back was about making amends to Nana because I let her down."

The ache emanating from deep inside of him caused tears to pool in her eyes. How she had misjudged him! This wasn't about vanity or mean-spiritedness. This was about grief and Hud's need to make amends to Lillian.

"There was no way you could have known she would pass away," Molly said. In this moment, she simply wanted to comfort him. He was hurting. Not only was he grieving Lillian's loss, but he hadn't forgiven himself for not being present when she passed away. The weight of his guilt seemed massive.

Tears shone in his eyes. "I should have been there, the way she was always there for me." He ran a shaky hand over his face. "I bought a plane ticket for the end of the week thinking I could rush to see her once I landed." His face crumpled. "But she died before I could make it home."

"Oh, Hud. I'm so sorry," she said. "I can't imagine how awful that must've been." All this time and she'd been judging him for not making it back to Serenity Peak to see Lillian.

He ducked his head and wouldn't meet her eyes. Raw emotion was overflowing from him. "I'm not sure I'll ever forgive myself. I was too ashamed and distraught to come home for the funeral. I know that might sound strange, but I was in such a bad place that I could barely think straight. And the guilt kept piling up, making me believe that I couldn't even show my face here in town."

How she wished someone had been able to help him at the time so that all of his emotions hadn't been able to fester. She imagined that his family had tried, but knowing Hud, he'd probably put up a wall.

She reached out and gripped his hand in hers. "It doesn't sound strange at all now that you've explained it. You were going through something that was extraordinarily painful. We all handle loss differently. There's no right or wrong."

"Thanks for saying that. I've convinced myself that everything I've done is wrong."

"When my gran died, I was stoic until November rolled around—her birthday month. And she wasn't around to celebrate. I fell apart," she confessed. "I thought that I was doing so well until that moment."

Hud met her eyes. "I feel badly that I never sent you a card or offered my condolences, but I'm so sorry about Eva. I know how much you loved her."

She nodded. "I wish that I'd reached out to you as well. We both had huge losses. We were both mourning. Yet a huge divide separated us."

Somehow they had lost the connection they'd shared. They had been childhood friends and then something more tender for a brief period. And in an instant, it had all vanished in a puff of smoke. Ten years had gone by without a single meaningful moment between them.

And now, she was remembering all the reasons why Hud had been so special to her. She had buried the memories of what he'd meant to her to spare herself hurt. And now, with Hud back in town, all the old feelings had come roaring back. She cared so much about this man.

"Coming back home…it's all about my grandmother and her legacy." His voice softened. "It's a way for me to make up for not being here. For letting her down."

Finally, she had a glimmer of understanding as to why Hud was trying to stake a claim on Humbled. Atonement. He felt as if he needed to make up for not being around when Lillian passed away. Because of her own personal experiences, Molly knew how important such moments were. Being robbed of them would cause a world of pain.

He drew a deep breath. "I—I'm feeling better now." He let out a harsh laugh. "Sorry for ruining this special evening."

"Hud, you didn't ruin a single thing. Honestly, this has been a spectacular evening." She leaned toward him. "The handsomest man in town called me beautiful. It doesn't get any better than that."

"You think I'm the most handsome man in town?" he asked, sounding incredulous.

"Oh, I wasn't talking about you," she teased. "Earlier tonight, Phineas told me that I'm beautiful."

Hud threw back his head and let loose with a chuckle. "Oh, Molly. You sure know how to make me laugh."

She chuckled along with him. "I'm glad." Hud needed a little relief from all of this angst.

He reached over and ran his fingers across her lips, gently tracing the outline of them.

"I'm so thankful for you. I'm not sure what I would do without you," he said in a low voice.

"Well, you're stuck with me, Hud Doherty." Although she kept her tone light, Molly meant every word. And she hoped that Hud knew it as well. Hud was never supposed to mean this much to her, yet he did. There wasn't a single thing Molly could do to put her feelings on ice.

Their gazes met and held. They both leaned in at the same time, their lips meeting in a searing kiss that left her a little breathless. Even though the night air was frigid, Molly almost didn't feel the cold as the kiss soared and deepened. Hud's lips were warm. He tasted like peppermint hot cocoa. She grabbed the collar of his parka and leaned against him.

The chatter of little voices interrupted them, causing them to pull apart. A group of kids around Theo's age must have seen their embrace. They were pointing in their direction and making oohing and aahing sounds.

"Molly and Hud sitting in a tree," they began to sing. "K-I-S-S-I-N-G. First comes love then comes marriage then comes baby in the baby carriage."

Molly jumped to her feet and called out. "I see you, Matty Gold. Lacey Shaw. George Locke. Harry Lee. I see all of you."

Just then a snowball hit Molly in the chest. She let out a cry of surprise as her parka was splattered by snow. "What in the world!" she shouted.

"Did they just hurl a snowball at you?" Hud asked, shaking his head. She wasn't sure he was as appalled as she was considering that he was on the verge of smiling.

"Yes, they did," Molly said. "And they're not getting away with it!"

Hud chuckled. "They're just kids, Molly. We did the same thing when we were their age."

She wagged a finger at him. "You may have done that, but I didn't," she protested. "Don't you remember? I was a Goody Two-shoes. These kids need to learn a lesson."

Whomp! A snowball hit Hud in his left arm. He began to sputter. "What's wrong with these kids? Once is mildly funny, but twice is a declaration of war." He bent over and picked up a clump of snow then formed it into the perfect snowball.

"Are we doing this?" Molly asked, invigorated by the spontaneity of the moment. The very idea of having a snowball fight made her feel like a little kid again.

"Of course we are," Hud said. "Let's go." With a wild roar, he took off in the direction of the kids, who were letting out screams and scrambling to throw more snowballs.

Molly, armed with a snowball in each hand, ran behind Hud, dodging snowballs and hurling a few of her own. Ten minutes later and the snowball fight was over, with Molly and Hud claiming victory.

"I can't believe we got beat by old people," Lacey muttered as the group walked away from the scene of the showdown.

Molly let out a hoot of laughter. "Did you hear that? We're old."

Hud let out a snort. "That's just sour grapes because we showed 'em a thing or two about snowball fights. We make a good team, Molly Truitt. And not just at Humbled and for snowball fights."

"We do," Molly said. She didn't want to read too much into Hud's words but they were music to her ears.

Hud dipped his head down and pressed a kiss against her lips.

At this moment, Molly didn't care who saw them kissing. This thing between her and Hud was exciting and unexpected. It was beginning to feel a lot like love.

By the time the tree lighting ceremony ended, Hudson was feeling a lot more settled about the events of the evening. Molly had made everything better with her compassion and kindness. She really was one of a kind. Last night had been telling in so many ways. His feelings for her were over-the-top, once-in-a-lifetime emotions. The thought of loving a woman had always terrified him. It was the very reason he'd left Serenity Peak so abruptly and ended things with Molly the first time around. His college plans had been in place for months thanks to Nana, but between Molly and his dad, Hud had chosen to cut his summer break short and leave Alaska.

But now, so much had changed.

He had changed. Because of Molly and all that she had brought to his world. Things were so great with them. The only issue that stood between them was Humbled. He had serious doubts about pursuing the lawsuit now due to his feelings for Molly, but of course that made him feel disloyal to Nana.

"Penny for your thoughts," Gramps said as he crept into the kitchen, where Hud was sitting at the table drinking hot cocoa and munching on sugar cookies. He had walked Molly home after the event and shared another romantic kiss with her.

"I'm just reflecting on tonight," Hud said. It had been full of ups and downs, but he and Molly had reconnected romantically. That was a huge development and a little bit overdue. He'd never been good at laying his feelings on the line, so this was a huge step.

"Everything okay with you? I noticed you left during the ceremony," Gramps said. His gaze was unwavering, and Hudson knew his grandfather wanted answers.

He took a swig of his hot chocolate. The sweet taste of the liquid instantly hit his taste buds. "I had a moment during the ceremony, Gramps. Everything came to a head regarding Nana's death. I haven't been dealing with it very well."

Bert sank down into the chair next to him. He placed his hand on the back of Hudson's neck. "Hey, there's no shame in that. We all process grief differently. Honestly, I'm going to grieve the loss of her for the rest of my days. It's okay to have bad moments."

"I've never forgiven myself for not being here," Hud said, his gaze focused on his mug.

"And I've never forgiven myself for not telling you about Lillian's heart condition. She swore me to secrecy. Had you known, I'm certain you would have rushed to her side."

"Don't blame yourself," Hud told him in a stern voice. "We could go back and forth over our regrets all night, and it wouldn't change anything. I didn't think twice about being made executor since you made the same request. Maybe I should have questioned the timing."

Gramps held up a finger. "Just remember, when things

seem overwhelming, it's always a good time to call on God. He won't ever fail you."

"Ever since I've come back I'm leaning on Him more and more. I'm not sure why, but I'm more grounded in my faith these days." Attending service at Serenity Peak church the other day had been a soulful experience. Hearing the women's choir perform had reminded him of attending Nana's performances and sitting in the front pew. The memory had served as a reminder that no matter how far away he'd strayed from his hometown, he was still a man of faith.

"That's what I love to hear. Nana would be proud of you."

His grandfather's words meant the world to him. All he'd ever wanted was for his family to think highly of him. Maybe now that he was home for good they could. Even his father, who didn't have much to say to him these days. They would have to hash out their differences before their divide became irreparable. That was the last thing Hud wanted.

"And what about you and Molly? From what I witnessed tonight, things seem to be progressing nicely between the two of you." There was a gleam in Gramps's eyes.

"I don't kiss and tell, but I'm a happy man," Hud said. Just thinking about Molly made him feel as if he could soar to the stratosphere.

"So when are you going to let the family know that your life in Boston wasn't all it was cracked up to be?" Bert reached for a sugar cookie and took a big bite of it.

Hudson narrowed his gaze as he studied his grandfather. "Now how did you know that? All I said was that it was complicated."

"Oh, Hud. You would have to wake up a lot earlier to pull the wool over my eyes." He let out a little laugh.

He splayed his hands on the table. "Okay, so I'll give

you the condensed version. My life in Boston wasn't nearly as glowing as I made it seem. I never enjoyed my job all that much, although it was fun coming up with marketing ideas. I hated the long hours and the lack of connection with my colleagues."

"Sounds stressful," Bert said. "Not the way I want you to live out your life."

"You and me both. I let things slide at work because I was unhappy with almost every single aspect of my life, and they let me go. Can't say I blame them. When you're miserable it shows in your work." He drummed his fingers on the table. "I'd been thinking a lot about Nana's legacy and how to cement it, so the timing was pretty perfect. Even if I'd wanted to, there was no way I could continue to live there without a job. And I didn't want to just get back on the hamster wheel with another job I hated."

"So is this your way of telling me that you love working at Humbled? I've noticed a certain spring in your step."

"Working at Humbled won't ever make me rich, Gramps. At least not monetarily. But it feeds my soul. And I've fallen in love with books again, just like I did when I was a kid."

Bert's face lit up. "You don't say! That's pretty cool." He leaned toward him so that their faces were close together. "Is Humbled the only thing you've fallen in love with?" He wiggled his eyebrows.

Just hearing Gramps say those words caused his stomach to clench. Falling in love wasn't for the faint of heart. It was thrilling and completely terrifying at the same time.

"You're absolutely incorrigible. You know that right?" Hudson asked.

"Right back atcha, grandson," Bert said with a wink. "It must be in our gene pool."

Chapter Sixteen

Molly looked at the calendar on the kitchen wall, marveling at how quickly time was passing by. Christmas was only a few days away, and her plans were still up in the air. She wanted to spend the day with Hud, but both of their families were hosting dinner. Even though their relationship was new, their history went back to the cradle. Their lives had been entwined for as long as Molly could remember. And with time ticking down it also served as a reminder that the thirty-day period would soon be up. She and Hud needed to talk and discuss the future. Molly needed to find out if he'd changed his mind about the lawsuit. That would truly be the best Christmas gift she'd ever received.

Humbled would be closed on Christmas and shutting down early on Christmas Eve. It would be a nice break for all of them. Today, as a little holiday surprise, she'd wrapped books in wrapping paper and placed a one paragraph description on the cover without naming the book. She was calling it blind dating with a book. The gifts would be placed at tables around the café as a little thank-you to customers for all of their support.

Molly's cell phone buzzed insistently in her apron pocket. She looked at the display, quickly picking up the call when she saw Phineas's name on the screen. It was a rare occasion when he contacted her during work hours. He knew the hectic pace at the shop didn't allow for many phone calls.

"Hey, Pops. Morning. What's going on?" she asked.

"Hey, Molly. Sorry to bother you during working hours, but I need to talk to you," Phineas said. "Any chance you can make time to chat with me after work?"

"Of course, Pops. Anything for you." It wasn't like Phineas to request her presence at his house. He never liked to ask for anything or make a fuss. This call made her antennas perk up.

"Bring Hudson," he said gruffly. Her grandfather's invite made her smile. Phineas seemed to like and respect Hud, which hadn't been the case a few weeks ago.

"He really is growing on you," she teased. Molly was happy that her grandfather had been able to see the great man underneath Hud's hard shell.

"There's something I need to share with the two of you. It's about the shop."

Her pulse skittered. It wasn't like her grandfather to request meetings. His tone sounded serious. He was usually more playful with her.

"Pops, you can't leave me hanging like this," Molly told him. "What's this all about?"

"Come tonight. All will be revealed," he said. His words sounded cryptic.

As she ended the call, Molly racked her brain trying to figure out why Pops wanted to talk to both her and Hud. Perhaps it was about Humbled and the lawsuit. Or maybe she was overthinking things. Gramps had gotten along well with Hud the last time they'd all been together.

Hopefully it was something positive. She didn't want to be at odds with the man she loved.

The realization still took her by surprise. She loved Hud. In the past, her feelings for him had been intense, but not like this. This was definitely love. A deep down to her soul love that had flourished against all odds. She hadn't even liked Hud a few weeks ago, yet now she couldn't imagine a world without him in it.

She entered the kitchen in search of him after not finding him in the café. He was using the blender and making a racket as he prepped drinks. When he turned it off, Molly made her presence known.

"I think you're wearing more of that mocha drink than you're serving," she told him. "Good thing you're wearing that apron."

Hud was wearing a moose-themed apron splattered with dark brown liquid. He was an adorable mess. Just the sight of him pulled at her heartstrings.

"I'm trying to get this recipe just right," he said, pouring the concoction into a small cup. He raised the drink to his lips and made a face after swallowing. "Nope. It's still a little off. Too bitter."

She loved his determination. It had taken her a long time to master the art of being a barista. So far, Hud had impressed her with his tenacity and grit. Whenever he made mistakes, he learned something from the experience.

"So, are you free tonight?" she asked him.

Hud raised his eyebrows. "What did you have in mind? Another snowball fight?"

She shook her head. "Not a chance," Molly said. "I've barely recovered from the last one... Phineas invited us over to his place after work. It sounds important." She hadn't been able to stop thinking about the phone call and the somber tone in her grandfather's voice. What was going on?

"Well then let's go. I don't think Phineas would invite

us out there if it wasn't something pressing." He sounded unbothered.

Molly appreciated Hud's willingness to meet up with her grandfather. Hud didn't seem all that curious about the invitation, which was a good thing. Maybe she was blowing it out of proportion. Was this her grandad's way of thanking Hud for being so kind the day he'd gotten himself locked in the basement? Maybe he'd planned something nice.

Or perhaps it *was* about the lawsuit.

She made it through the day on pins and needles. Molly had no idea why she was so rattled, but some instinct warned her that something was up. There was no point in her worrying Hud about it or making herself appear high strung. At the end of their shift, she and Hud took separate vehicles over to Phineas's house since Molly planned to stay for a bit and visit with her parents, who were back in town.

The moment they stepped into her grandfather's home, they both took their boots off so they didn't track snow into the house. Molly knew he'd been baking. Cinnamon and vanilla wafted through the air. Her mouth watered in anticipation of tasting his baked goods. He and her gran had taught her everything she knew about baking.

A few Christmas decorations had been added to the ones they'd put up during their last visit. The home looked cheery and festive. A small tree sat in the corner, adorned with vintage ornaments that had belonged to generations of her family.

"Come on through," Phineas called out. He was sitting at his kitchen table with plates of cookies laid out before him. Molly rushed toward him and placed a kiss on his grizzled cheek.

"Take a load off and help yourselves to my freshly baked cookies. I've been on a baking spree. If you'd like something to drink, I can put the kettle on." Molly easily recognized the cookies—snickerdoodles, gingerbread cookies and pecan balls.

"He was always the best baker in the family," Molly told Hud. "I learned the tricks of the trade from him." Memories of baking in this very kitchen with her grandparents surrounded her. They had always made Christmas cookies for the church cookie exchange. Their batches had always been sought after and raved about by the parishioners.

Hud bit into a snickerdoodle and let out a satisfied sound. "Now these should be on the menu at the café. They would sell out in a flash."

"How about you come out of retirement and join us, Pops?" Molly teased.

Phineas rolled his eyes and scoffed at the idea, but Molly could tell he was flattered. He and Gran had always baked with love, and she knew he must miss their partnership, especially during the holidays.

"Well, I'm sure you're wondering why you've been summoned," Phineas said, looking back and forth between them. His silver brows were furrowed.

"I have been wondering," Molly admitted as she helped herself to a pecan ball. Just biting into it and tasting the nutty flavor reminded her of hearth and home.

"It's all about these letters," Pops said, placing his palm on top of a stack of stationary. "I hadn't been ready to go through your gran's letters. I thought it would be too emotional, especially since my love letters to her are here. When Hudson brought up the Christmas boxes, this box of Eva's correspondence was among them." He gently smiled. "So I dug in once I realized what they were. I'm seeing them for the first time. I figured reading them might shed some light on things. Reading them has been quite a journey of the heart."

She reached out and patted his hand. "I'm sure it's been incredibly emotional."

He blinked back the moisture in his eyes. "It has been, but at times it made me feel closer than ever to my love. And that's a good thing."

Molly's gaze homed in on the stack of letters on the table. "Is there something in particular you found?"

"Some things I never really knew," Phineas told them. "Eva and Lillian were fiercely loyal to one another and spoke their own language. Even though they're no longer with us, your grandmothers are still revealing things to us."

"That's a good thing, right?" Hud asked. Up until this point, he'd been fairly quiet, simply listening and observing.

Phineas nodded. "I think truth is always powerful, even if it stings."

Molly and Hud exchanged a glance. She sensed that something monumental was coming. Goosebumps popped up on the back of her neck. Phineas wasn't one to play games. He was a straight shooter to his core.

"Tell us," Hud said, his voice gravelly.

Phineas drew in a deep breath. "Eva and Lillian exchanged dozens of letters over the years. In good times and in bad their deep bond was unbreakable."

"That's how I remember them," Molly said. An image popped into her head of two sweet-faced, silver-haired women who were joined at the hip.

"Before I read to you, I'm going to tell you that there was a period where they were estranged, fifteen years or so ago," Phineas explained. "They had some bumpy times."

"Over Humbled?" Hud asked. He was leaning across the table, looking intense.

Phineas nodded. "In part, but sometimes friends just have growing pains. It never made them love each other any less. They were like sisters. Squabbles. Bickering in the morning and having made up by lunchtime. Abiding love and friendship."

He focused his attention on Hud. "I know you believe that Lillian deserved co-ownership status at Humbled."

"Yes, I do. From everything I've seen and studied, she was a co-creator," Hud said.

"Then this letter is of vital importance." He reached for a blue envelope with faded ink. Phineas pulled out a letter written on cream-colored stationary. He cleared his throat then began to read.

"Dear Eva,
I've missed you. Words can't express how sorry I am that I let so much time go by before writing to you. I let my pride get in the way of our friendship. That deeply pains me. We both can be so prideful. I was so angry with you for my own choices. You asked me to partner with you in the shop, and I flat-out turned you down. I felt that my family needed me more than you did during that time. Bert and I waited so long for God to give us children I wanted to focus on being a mother.

I let the chance to be a part of the shop pass me by. And then I regretted it. It tore me up inside, and I lashed out.

No matter what, you're my best friend in this entire world. Let's meet for lunch and go from there.
Love,
Lillian"

Molly exhaled the deep breath she'd been holding. The letter was revealing in so many ways. Lillian and Eva's friendship had been stronger than any of their issues. If Hud had been seeking clarity, this was it.

And judging by the angry expression etched on his face, he was upset about the truth being uncovered, even though it was something he couldn't ignore.

Phineas tapped his fingers on the table. "So you see, it's all here in black and white."

"They made amends about the shop," Molly said, sounding as dazed as he felt. "Lillian let it go. And their friendship stayed intact."

Although he understood the implications of the letter, he was finding it hard to wrap his head around it. From everything he'd ever known, Nana had struggled once Humbled had flourished. Even if she'd accepted the situation, why hadn't the Truitts acknowledged her contributions?

"So, you're saying she just accepted the fact that she wasn't being given credit for all she'd done for Humbled?" Hud asked. He could hear the sharp edge in his voice, but he was past the point of pretending he wasn't upset. Everything he had believed to be true was falling apart. His head was pounding, and his palms were moist.

"Hud, I'm not saying a thing. Those were Lillian's words. I simply wanted you both to know that this existed," Phineas explained.

He knew what he'd heard, but it simply didn't compute.

"But wait. Abel said that my grandparents thought about taking this to court," Hud said. "That speaks volumes."

"Yes, that's what I heard back then. But they changed their minds and settled the issue out of court." Phineas shook the thin piece of paper. "I believe this letter sheds some light on why they let it go. Lillian acknowledged that she turned down the offer and made peace with it."

Hudson ran a shaky hand over his face. "But Gramps still believes that Nana was cheated out of co-ownership. He's told me so dozens of times over the years." He had journals, diary entries and photographs all pointing toward Nana's massive contributions to Humbled. Didn't that mean anything?

"That's understandable," Phineas said, scratching his jaw. "Bert sought to protect his wife and her wounded feelings. I would have done the same for my Eva. That's what husbands do."

Wounded feelings? That was what this had been all about? What about all the work Lillian had done to make Humbled a success? Her hard work and initiative. Didn't any of those things matter? Molly and Phineas were looking at him with a mixture of pity and confusion. Didn't they understand why he was so upset?

He threw his hands in the air. "So that's it?"

How could something so monumental be reduced to a few lines in a letter? Working at Humbled had made him feel so connected to Nana and Molly. Surely that had to have meant something.

"This makes no sense," he muttered. At the moment, he was having trouble processing this information. Just when he'd thought things were going so well at Humbled and with his return to Serenity Peak, he'd been blindsided.

"If it makes you feel better, the Lillian sandwich was an homage to your grandmother," Phineas explained. "Eva wanted to honor her in a meaningful way."

Hudson let out a snort. "An egg sandwich is meaningful? For someone who helped create the business! I have photos of her working side by side with Eva. Her journals detailed everything she did along the way. She was there during the ground breaking and the construction. She was there for all of it!"

"Hud," Molly said, gripping his arm. "Calm down. I know this isn't easy to hear, but lashing out isn't the answer."

"You're right, Hud," Phineas said. "She was truly a helper. But she was there as a friend and a support system, not as a co-owner. I've always known that based on what I witnessed, but I think it's important to see it in writing. In a court of law that would be proof."

"So you're saying that I don't have any standing. Right?" Hud asked. Even though he already knew the answer, he wanted to hear Phineas say it.

"In my humble opinion, Hudson, you don't," Phineas told him. He twisted his mouth, appearing regretful. "I know this must be disappointing."

Disappointing didn't even come close to what he was experiencing. What a fool he'd been. All this time, he'd believed that he could ride to the rescue and right a terrible wrong. This had all blown up in his face. It was over.

"If it makes you feel any better, I wasn't privy to most of this," Phineas said. "And I don't think Bert was either. Those two ladies were as thick as thieves, and they kept a lot of this between them."

Hudson scoffed. "Actually there's not much that can make me feel better right now."

"Let's keep talking this out," Molly suggested. "We can find a way to wade through this…together."

He knew none of this was Molly's fault, but he didn't want to hear her spin on things. She'd won after all, and he had lost. His big lofty goal had crashed and burned.

"Why? There's nothing more to be said," Hudson spit

out. "Molly, you have my resignation from Humbled, effective immediately."

Molly let out a gasp. "No, Hud. That's not the answer. Take a deep breath."

How could he when he could barely breathe at all.

He jumped up from his chair and grabbed his coat and keys. It took him a moment to jam his boots on his feet. Thankfully, he and Molly had taken separate vehicles. He needed to get as far away from this place as possible.

Seconds later, he heard footsteps crunching in the snow behind him.

"Hud!" Molly called out. "Wait!"

Before he could make it to his vehicle, he felt Molly tugging on his parka. He whirled around to face her. He held up his hands. "Molly, I can't do this. Not right now."

"Talk to me. Believe it or not, I understand what you're feeling."

"How could you possibly understand? I didn't just do all of this on a whim. I truly believed that I was doing the right thing. And now I have nothing." Everything had slipped away from him in one fell swoop. The opportunity to carve out a legacy for Nana. To make the entire town value Lillian's contributions. To show the Truitts that they'd been wrong this entire time. Now, none of this would come to pass.

"That's not true. You have *me*, Hud."

A few hours ago, he would have given anything to hear those words come out of her mouth. Yet, at the moment, her words fell flat. He was operating on autopilot. A big part of him had shut down.

"Hud, we could still work together," Molly pleaded. "We make a pretty good team, don't we?"

What was she trying to prove? He wasn't in any position to think about anything other than the fact that he'd been chasing fool's gold. His dream of creating a legacy for his grandmother was over. Finished. His future in Serenity Peak was looking bleak.

"No," he said, wrenching his arm away from her grasp. "I don't want your charity or pity. You're off the hook now. You don't have to humor me by working with me."

"You're talking nonsense. Don't let your pain blind you to what's standing right in front of you."

So much anger and grief had been building up inside of him, making him feel as if he might explode.

"There's nothing left for me here. Don't you get it? I failed again."

"Hud, don't you see? This has nothing to do with anything you did or didn't do. You can't keep blaming yourself for everything under the sun," Molly said fiercely.

What was left for him now? He'd given up his life in Boston for a wild-goose chase. He had no legal claim to Humbled. He had failed in his efforts to honor Nana. And he'd made a fool of himself in the process. How could anyone take him seriously ever again? He wasn't sure he could even look at himself in the mirror.

"I'm done, Molly. With everything. It's that simple." His voice sounded flat. For all intents and purposes, he had emotionally checked out.

"So you're just going to give up on everything, including us?" He could see the hurt in her eyes, and it gutted him. In a perfect world, he would reach out and take her in his arms. Console her. Hudson would tell her that nothing mattered as long as they were together. But the words died in his throat, snuffed out by the harsh reality of Phineas's revelation.

He shrugged, allowing the empty feelings to consume him. "I'm not sure there ever really was an us, Molly."

Hudson got into his vehicle and revved the engine, roaring away from the property as the twinkling Christmas lights shimmered in his rearview mirror. He could make out Molly standing exactly where he'd left her, looking just as broken as Hudson felt.

Chapter Seventeen

Molly couldn't remember a time when she'd felt so low. Even though Christmas Eve was supposed to be filled with cheer and happy tidings, she didn't feel joyful. The scene with Hud at her grandfather's home kept replaying in her head like a bad recurring dream.

There's nothing left for me here.

I'm not sure there ever really was an us, Molly.

His words had absolutely broken her heart. Her head kept telling her that he hadn't meant what he'd said, but her heart wasn't so sure. All of the old insecurities over their past relationship came flooding back to her. Maybe he had been simply speaking his truths. And perhaps love wasn't something that was meant to be for her. So far all she'd experienced was heartache.

After his brutal parting words, Molly had gone back inside and broken down in her grandfather's arms. She'd sobbed like a baby, allowing Pops to pat her back and console her the way he'd done when she was little.

"Don't worry, Molly girl. He's just hurt and feeling a little off-kilter," he whispered in her ear.

"You didn't hear him outside. He sounded broken," she told him.

"It's hard when you feel as if all is lost. He's fallen down, but if he's the man I think he is, he'll pick himself up and carry on."

Oh, how she wished it would come to pass. Not having Hud at Humbled would be a hardship. Not having him in her life would leave a huge hole in her heart. She had grown to rely on him in ways she couldn't even express. He was everything to her. A partner in crime. A confidante. The love of her life. If he packed up and left town again, she didn't think she would ever get over it, even at one hundred years old.

Showing up this morning at Humbled and knowing Hud wouldn't be there had filled her with absolute dread. She'd grown used to the sound of his laughter and the charm he had on full display when dealing with customers. She couldn't walk into the kitchen without images of him making a huge mess with the blender flashing before her eyes. Hud was everywhere in Humbled. He was in the pages of the books he'd shelved. He was in every square inch of the property.

That was when it dawned on her that this was how he'd felt about his grandmother's presence at the shop.

All this time, she hadn't wanted to acknowledge the fact that Hud might've been right. It was all she could think about now. Lillian and Eva had been best friends. Lillian had assisted with ideas for the shop and been involved from the ground up. Had her family cheated Lillian out of the opportunity? She would never believe that to be the truth, but now she was forced to examine what was right. What was Lillian owed? As a woman of faith and a believer, Molly knew in her heart what the answer was.

Molly was so deep in her thoughts that she hadn't heard Estelle sneak up on her in the kitchen.

"So, Hud really isn't coming back?" Estelle asked her.

Her friend's feelings were stamped all over her face. Estelle had been upset earlier when Molly had told her about what had transpired with Hud at her grandfather's place.

Molly shook her head. "Hud made it clear that he was done with Humbled and everything else in this town."

Her eyes widened. "Surely that doesn't include you," Estelle said. "The two of you have grown so close. It's been such a pleasure watching you two connect."

"I thought—" Molly's mouth dried up. How could she explain that all of her hopes and dreams for the future had become tied up in Hud? She didn't want to sound ridiculous or weak, as if she needed a man to be able to breathe oxygen. But she had dared to dream of merging business success with personal happiness with Hud.

Estelle reached out and squeezed her hand. "You thought that the two of you had a future together. Am I right?"

"Yes," she said in a soft voice as hot tears landed on her cheeks. "He came back to Serenity Peak with a desire for vengeance, but that all shifted when we began working together. He showed me that he's a good man. I really thought that this time we would go the distance."

"And you still might," Estelle encouraged. "Don't give up on him, Molly. This is just one hurdle that you need to vault over."

"I'm not the one giving up," she said. "He's the one who seems to have thrown in the towel. And nothing I said to him seemed to register at all."

"He was in shock. Maybe in denial too. It's hard to give up on a narrative that you've been playing over and over in your head," Estelle said. "Molly, I'm going to give you some unsolicited advice. Many years ago, I made a huge mistake. I allowed pride to stop me from going after the man I loved." She closed her eyes for a moment. "His name was Brock, and we were high school sweethearts. He was the love of my life, and I let him slip through my fingers. Take it from me. You'll regret it for the rest of your life if you don't."

Molly could hear the pain laced in Estelle's voice. She had always wondered why a kind and lovely woman like Estelle was single. Now she knew. And she didn't want that to happen to her and Hud. She knew that he had feelings for her despite the things he'd said. It hadn't all been a figment of her imagination. Molly had felt it in his kisses and the way he'd swept his palm across her cheek. They had shared moments of amazing chemistry.

"Go to him!" Estelle urged her. "Before it's too late."

Estelle was right! She needed to find Hud and tell him everything that was laying on her heart. She was so afraid that he was going to do something rash like leave town and go back to Boston. That would absolutely crush her. And considering the way he'd been talking…

Most likely he wouldn't leave before spending Christmas with his family. Tonight was the Christmas Eve party at the Doherty Tree Farm. He'd invited her weeks ago, before their recent dust up. Although she figured Hud wouldn't want her in attendance, he was about to get a big surprise. There was so much resting on her heart that she needed to tell him.

She was going to scream it from the rooftops if need be. Hud Doherty was going to listen to what she had to say. And she was going to make him see what was right in front of him. She loved him! And if he wasn't being so short sighted, he would realize that they had a future together.

She grabbed her friend by her arms. "Estelle, help me close up the shop. I've got to get ready for a Christmas Eve party at the Doherty Tree Farm."

"That's what I'm talking about," Estelle said, jumping up and down. "I'm ready and able if you need a wing woman."

"I could definitely use the moral support," Molly said, leaning in for a hug.

"Don't you worry, Molly," Estelle said. "You've got this!"

Although Molly was buoyed by her friend's support, she was still nervous about Operation Hud. The stakes were extremely high.

After all, her heart was on the line.

The Doherty Tree Farm had never looked better. Every row of trees had twinkling lights that illuminated the area. Flameless candles had been strewn along the walkway, lighting a path for the guests. Tureens of warm soup, mac and cheese, and cocoa greeted folks as they entered. His family had set up a fun photo booth so folks could memorialize the event. Vivid red poinsettias were in abundance at the gathering. One for each guest to take home as a favor.

Normally, Hud would be in the thick of things, enjoying the evening with his family and friends. He kept looking for Molly whenever someone walked in.

Why would she show up? he asked himself. He'd been awful to her, saying hurtful things that he hadn't meant. Hud had never been the best at finding the right words to express himself. He was struggling to find a way to reach out to Molly. Perhaps he just needed some time to get himself together. Wanting to lick his wounds in private, Hud headed over to the shed where his father and Gramps had their workshop. It was one of Hud's favorite places due to the smell of cedar and sawdust. He sat down in the vintage rocking chair one of his ancestors had handcrafted. At the moment, solitude felt like a nice warm blanket wrapped around him.

The creaking sound of the door opening alerted him to the fact that he was no longer alone. His father was standing in the doorway staring at him.

"Son, I wanted to check in with you. You've been awfully quiet the last few days," his father noted. "You've got everyone worried, especially your mother."

"No need to worry. I'm all right," he said. Even though he wasn't. He suspected his father knew he wasn't telling the truth.

Jordy came closer and sat down on a wooden bench a few feet away from him. Hud couldn't think of the last time they had been alone together. "Do you want to talk?" he asked.

Hud blew out a deep breath. "I don't know what good it'll do. I came back home thinking I could do something great for Nana's legacy, and it all blew up in my face." He got his dad up to speed on the letter Lillian had sent to Eva.

Jordy ran a hand over his face and sighed. "That's a tough break. I know your intentions were pure, but the situation was always muddled."

"Tell me about it," Hud muttered. "I feel like I've been wading in pea soup."

His father twisted his lips. "For what it's worth, I'm happy you're back. It gutted me when you left and moved so far away. I know that I was a part of the reason you wanted to get away from Serenity Peak, and I'm sorry for that." He wasn't used to him being so open and vulnerable. Maybe there was hope for their relationship after all.

"You weren't the only reason," Hud said. "I was eighteen with growing pains. I didn't want to spend the rest of my life in small-town Alaska."

Jordy nodded. "I get it now. But at the time it really hurt me."

"I had no idea," he admitted. "For so long, it seemed like you didn't like me very much. And that really hurt me."

A look of shock passed over his face. "Hud, you're my firstborn child. I love you to the ends of the earth, and I always will."

His father came over and enveloped him in a tight bear hug. When they pulled apart, Jordy regarded him with sharp eyes. "And is it really Humbled that's bothering you? Or is it Molly?"

"At the end of the day, Humbled is a shop. Molly, on the other hand, means the world to me. And I really said some hurtful things to her." He winced. "I can't imagine her ever forgiving me for how I acted."

"Your faith has taught you better than that, son. Love bears all things," he said, paraphrasing Corinthians. "If you love her, fight for her."

"I do love her," he said. "Living without Molly isn't an option. And I want to fight to earn her forgiveness."

"Then what are you doing here? Go find her!" Jordy said.

"I will. I am," Hud said, standing up and checking his pockets for his keys. He took off toward the driveway at breakneck speed, fueled by his father's encouragement.

The glare of headlights in the driveway momentarily blinded him. He held his arm up across his eyes, irritated by the truck blocking his way. Seconds later, the driver parked and stepped out into his line of sight.

"Molly!" he said, blown away by the sight of her.

"Hud!" she said. "Are you going somewhere?"

"Not anymore. I was coming to find you," he said. "What are you doing here?"

"I came to find you," Molly said. She advanced toward

him. "I'm going to talk, and you're going to listen!" She jabbed a finger in his chest.

"Ouch! Okay, I'm listening," he said, bracing for her to tell him off. He absolutely deserved it. He had to admit that he liked this fiery side of her.

"You didn't listen to a word I had to say the other day. All you wanted to do was wallow in your own pain and disappointment. You made me an afterthought." She paused to take a breath. "We're a team, Hud. And you lost sight of that."

Her words pierced his insides. He didn't think that he could feel worse about the situation, but he'd been wrong.

"I shouldn't have stormed off like that," Hud said, meeting Molly's gaze. "I was prideful and foolish."

"You're right. You shouldn't have acted out, but I understand," she told him.

That was just like Molly. He'd behaved badly, and she was full of compassion and grace. Hudson was going to do his best to explain things to her. Maybe she had room in her heart for forgiveness. If it meant they could be together, he would go to any lengths to make her understand. "It might sound ridiculous, but when Phineas read my grandmother's letter to us, it felt like everything was slipping away from me."

"Everything? Or Humbled?" she asked.

The glint in her eyes told him that he needed to choose his words wisely. "I've thought a lot about it, Molly. It's not about Humbled. To prove it, I'm tossing out the lawsuit. It's a done deal. Honestly, it was always about what Humbled represents, most of all the chance for redemption. I wanted so badly to make amends to Nana for not being there when she passed. I thought that I could honor her in that way, but the truth is, I wanted this ache inside me to heal. And part of that journey is coming to the realization that there are other ways to honor her."

"Oh, Hud. You've been through so much." She reached out and gripped his hand.

"What I've come to realize is that loving you has done more to heal me than anything else. You are what matters to me most."

Molly's mouth hung open. "You love me?"

He placed his hands on the sides of her face and looked deeply into her eyes. He knew that she would be able to see love radiating from his gaze. All he needed was her unwavering love. "Yes, Molly Truitt. I'm madly in love with you. I think that I always have been, going all the way back to the sandbox."

"I love you too, Hud. And I remember playing with you in that sandbox. You were relentless about pulling my pigtails," she said.

"That was my love language," Hud said, chuckling. "And my way of getting your attention."

"You don't ever have to worry about that. You'll always be the focus of my world, Hud Doherty." She tilted her face up so that he could kiss her. He didn't disappoint her. And God willing, he never would.

Epilogue

One year later

"I think this is the perfect tree," Molly announced. She stood back and surveyed the six-foot pine tree that she knew would look spectacular at Humbled. Once they dressed it up with ornaments and tinsel, the tree would look even more breathtaking. This holiday season was shaping up to be wonderful, full of love and light. So much had changed in the past year. Humbled now had a plaque in Lillian's honor in the bookstore, which would forever memorialize her contributions to the business. Both their families had rejoiced over the lawsuit being tossed out. The future looked bright.

Hud folded his arms across his chest and eyeballed the tree. "Are you sure?"

"Of course I'm sure. I absolutely love it."

"If you love it, then so do I." Hud stood behind her and wrapped his arms around her middle. They stood there for a moment admiring the tree at Hud's family's tree farm. There was so much to look forward to during the most special time of the year. Humbled was the place where she and Hud had fallen in love and managed to honor both of their grandmothers' legacies. Business was doing well, and thanks to their brainstorming sessions, new events were always on the calendar. They were fulfilling their own dreams as well as their grandmothers'.

She turned around so they were standing face-to-face. "That makes me very happy. I hope you are too."

He nodded, looking down at her with an enraptured expression.

"I love how you're one of the only people who calls me Hud." He placed a tender kiss on her lips. "I love how your eyes shimmer more than a fully lit Christmas tree." He reached out and swept his hand across her face, brushing her hair to the side. "And most of all, I love how you care for others, even scoundrels like me."

"You're a reformed scoundrel, Hud Doherty," she teased. "There's a difference."

"The love of a good woman works wonders," he said, running his knuckles against her jawline.

"I do love you, Hud. More than I ever imagined possible." The last year had been transformative, full of professional and personal highs. Working alongside Hud and falling in love with him had been amazing. She had never imagined for a single moment that his return would yield such happiness.

"And I love you too, my sweet Molly. The last year has been the most wonderful of my entire life. Coming back home was meant to be." He dipped his head down and placed a kiss on her temple.

"I wish that our grans had been here to witness us falling in love." Tears misted her eyes. Losing her gran was still a painful loss, but, along with Hud, she'd decided to embrace the spirit of the season and live her best life.

"But I truly believe they're both smiling down on us," Hud said.

Molly nodded, knowing he was right. The ones we love never truly left us. Love endured.

"We make an amazing pair, don't we?" Molly asked. "If I say so myself."

He made a face. "I think things could be better."

She frowned at him. Better? Her heart began to beat a bit faster than normal.

"We've already shown that we can work together to tackle hard issues," Hud told her. "We overcame our differences and chose to see each other in the best light."

She nodded. "We gave each other grace, and I'll always be grateful for that."

"Well," Hud said, "I wanted to kickstart this holiday season with something very special to show you just how much you mean to me."

"Oh," she said, pressing her mittened hand against her chest. His words gave her the warm fuzzies. "An early Christmas gift. How sweet."

"That all depends on if you accept the gift," Hud said, winking at her.

Why is he talking in riddles? Before she could ask, Hud was down on bended knee in front of her, holding out a ring in an antique wooden box. She let out a little squeal then covered her mouth. Hudson grinned up at her, his handsome features illuminated by the full moon.

"Molly Truitt, you've changed my world in so many ways I can't even express. You inspire me to be better, to do better. When I first came back to Serenity Peak, I was consumed by anger and bitterness. Because of you, I came to the realization that love is stronger than pride. I can't imagine walking through life with anyone else but you."

Tears were now falling freely down her face.

"Molly, will you join me in this journey called life? I

promise to have and to hold, to honor you all the days of my life."

"Yes, Hud," Molly said, falling to her knees in the snow. "I can't imagine a life without you in it."

"I was hoping you would say that," Hud said, reaching for her hand and tugging off the mitten. He then took her ring finger and slid on the brilliant diamond. Molly looked down at it, admiring the round cut stone surrounded by smaller diamonds. She couldn't recall ever seeing such a spectacular ring.

"This ring is stunning, Hud," she said. "There's something almost vintage about it."

Hud rose to a standing position, pulling her along with him. "It was my grandmother's ring. Gramps gave it to me a few months ago. I guess he knew before I did that I wanted to propose," he said grinning.

"Bert is a very smart man," Molly said, holding her ring finger up in the air. "With extremely good taste in diamond rings. I'm so honored to be wearing Lillian's ring."

"I'm pretty smart too," Hud said, "because I know that you're the only woman for me."

"I better be," Molly teased, gently swatting him with her hand. "After all, I'm going to be your wife."

"Should we go tell my family?" Hud asked, looking over at the Doherty house. The place was lit up with twinkling lights on the outside and a soft glow emanating from inside the home.

"If you don't mind, can we keep this as our little secret for a while?" Molly asked. "I just want the two of us to savor this amazing news. Only for a little bit, then we can shout it from the rooftops."

"I like the sound of that," Hud said, encircling her waist with his hands and pulling her against his chest.

"Kiss me, my love," Molly said, looking up at him with stars in her eyes. At that moment, he thought she was the most beautiful woman he'd ever seen. And she was his. He wasn't afraid this time to love her with all of his heart. The only thing that would ever frighten him was the idea of losing her.

As the snow gently fell down among the rows and rows of Christmas trees, Hud placed a triumphant kiss on Molly's lips. It signified their glorious future and the love that had flourished between them.

They both knew without a doubt that this was the beginning of forever.

* * * * *

*If you enjoyed this story,
discover more delightful books in*
New York Times *bestselling author
Belle Calhoune's series,
Serenity Peak
Available now from Love Inspired!*

Dear Reader,

Thank you for joining me on another journey to Serenity Peak, Alaska. I've enjoyed writing Molly and Hud's love story. I love the childhood-friend-to-romance trope. They share a rich and complicated history that deepens their connection despite a few bumps in the road. Both Molly and Hud are trying their best to uphold the legacies of their grandmothers. Grappling with the loss of a loved one is one of the themes of this book, as well as forgiving oneself. Hud grapples with a lot of guilt, and he must deal with it in order to have a future with Molly.

There's something about a café-bookstore that I find to be so charming. What could be better than ordering your favorite coffee drink and baked good then perusing the bookshelves? If I could choose an alternate career, I would love to own a shop like Humbled.

It's a pleasure to write for the Harlequin Love Inspired line. Working at home in my pajamas is a wonderful perk of the job. I can be found online at my Author Belle Calhoune Facebook page, and you can sign up for my newsletter via my website, bellecalhoune.com

Blessings,
Belle

From Alaska with Love Spice Cake

One heart-shaped Bundt pan

Ingredients:

- 4 eggs, separated
- ½ pound of butter, softened
- 2 cups sugar
- 1 tsp vanilla extract
- 2 ½ cups cake flour
- 2 tsp baking powder
- ¼ tsp salt
- 1 ½ tsp nutmeg
- 3 tsp cinnamon
- 1 tsp ground cloves
- 1 cup buttermilk

Preheat oven to 350°F.

Grease and flour baking pan.

Using electric mixer with whisk attachment, beat egg whites until stiff and set aside.

Using electric mixer at medium speed, cream the butter.

Add the sugar and mix until light in color. Add vanilla. Add egg yolks one at a time, beating well after each one.

In a separate bowl, combine flour, baking powder, salt, nutmeg, cinnamon and cloves. Add this mixture to the egg yolk mixture, alternating with the buttermilk. Start and end with flour mixture. Blend until batter is smooth. Gently fold mixture into egg whites.

Pour batter into pan. Bake for 25 to 30 minutes. After cake cools, sprinkle powdered sugar on top or spread frosting if desired.

Recipe from Sierra Calhoune

Get up to 4 Free Books!

We'll send you 2 free books from each series you try PLUS a free Mystery Gift.

FREE Value Over $25

Both the **Love Inspired** and **Love Inspired** Suspense series feature compelling novels filled with inspirational romance, faith, forgiveness and hope.

YES! Please send me 2 FREE novels from the Love Inspired or Love Inspired Suspense series and my FREE gift (gift is worth about $10 retail). After receiving them, if I don't wish to receive any more books, I can return the shipping statement marked "cancel." If I don't cancel, I will receive 6 brand-new Love Inspired Larger-Print books or Love Inspired Suspense Larger-Print books every month and be billed just $7.19 each in the U.S. or $7.99 each in Canada. That is a savings of 20% off the cover price. It's quite a bargain! Shipping and handling is just 50¢ per book in the U.S. and $1.25 per book in Canada.* I understand that accepting the 2 free books and gift places me under no obligation to buy anything. I can always return a shipment and cancel at any time by calling the number below. The free books and gift are mine to keep no matter what I decide.

Choose one:
☐ **Love Inspired Larger-Print** (122/322 BPA G36Y)
☐ **Love Inspired Suspense Larger-Print** (107/307 BPA G36Y)
☐ **Or Try Both!** (122/322 & 107/307 BPA G36Z)

Name (please print)

Address   Apt. #

City   State/Province   Zip/Postal Code

Email: Please check this box ☐ if you would like to receive newsletters and promotional emails from Harlequin Enterprises ULC and its affiliates. You can unsubscribe anytime.

Mail to the **Harlequin Reader Service:**
IN U.S.A.: P.O. Box 1341, Buffalo, NY 14240-8531
IN CANADA: P.O. Box 603, Fort Erie, Ontario L2A 5X3

Want to explore our other series or interested in ebooks? **Visit www.ReaderService.com or call 1-800-873-8635.**

---

*Terms and prices subject to change without notice. Prices do not include sales taxes, which will be charged (if applicable) based on your state or country of residence. Canadian residents will be charged applicable taxes. Offer not valid in Quebec. This offer is limited to one order per household. Books received may not be as shown. Not valid for current subscribers to the Love Inspired or Love Inspired Suspense series. All orders subject to approval. Credit or debit balances in a customer's account(s) may be offset by any other outstanding balance owed by or to the customer. Please allow 4 to 6 weeks for delivery. Offer available while quantities last.

Your Privacy—Your information is being collected by Harlequin Enterprises ULC, operating as Harlequin Reader Service. For a complete summary of the information we collect, how we use this information and to whom it is disclosed, please visit our privacy notice located at https://corporate.harlequin.com/privacy-notice. Notice to California Residents – Under California law, you have specific rights to control and access your data. For more information on these rights and how to exercise them, visit https://corporate.harlequin.com/california-privacy. For additional information for residents of other U.S. states that provide their residents with certain rights with respect to personal data, visit https://corporate.harlequin.com/other-state-residents-privacy-rights/.

LIRLIS25